GRRRLS ON THE SIDE

CARRIE PACK

interlude press • new york

ISBN 13: 978-1-945053-21-4 (trade)
ISBN 13: 978-1-945053-37-5(ebook)
Published by Duet, an imprint of Interlude Press
www.duetbooks.com

Book and Cover Design by CB Messer
Book Photography ©Depositphotos.com/applea/MartiniDry/different_nata/ABBPhoto/whynotme.cz/Ksania/verywell/IgorBukhlin/creatista/stokkete/AntonioGuillemF/pxhidalgo/dstaerk/Amelie1/Sashatigar/Katja87/c-foto
10 9 8 7 6 5 4 3 2 1

interlude press • new york

To all Riot Grrrls, past, present and future.

"The early '90s were a difficult time to be a woman, especially a young one, and too little has changed in the intervening decades."

—Sara Marcus, *Girls to the Front: The True Story of the Riot Grrrl Revolution*

AUTHOR'S NOTE

Riot Grrrl was a moment in time that represented what being young and female meant within the greater context of our society. It also helped a lot of us to understand what was possible. Many of us knew that even though significant strides had been made for gender and racial equality, the world was far from equal. In the early 1990s, a group of socially aware young women created (some would argue that they stumbled upon) a feminist movement they dubbed Riot Grrrl.

When I starting writing *Grrrls on the Side* more than a year ago, the world was a different place for women. As we approached the 2016 election, it seemed we were on the cusp of having our first female president. Progress had been made. Our voices were being heard. I had nostalgia for Riot Grrrl. The moment felt ripe for a book that reflected on how far we've come as feminists and the role that young women and girls have played in that journey. Now, I believe, this book may have a different purpose. I sincerely hope *Grrrls* serves as a reminder of the power that women carry within ourselves, of the joy, kindness and ferocity we bring to everything we do, and of the hope that it can and will get better because we have each other.

With the historic Women's March on Washington in January 2017, I once again saw the power of women and girls to influence change on a grand scale. We still have a long way to go, but there are always other women out there, fighting the good fight, who will stand up and have your back, who will call you out on your crap, and who will remind you that you are not alone.

So thank you so much for giving *Grrrls on the Side* a chance. Tabitha's story represents a journey that a lot of young women take on their path to finding their place in the world, and I believe that is an important message for young adults. Unfortunately, for one in six American women, that journey is often derailed by sexual assault[1]. So it would be impossible to talk about feminism and Riot Grrrl without addressing that very real and important issue.

While there are no specific depictions of rape in my novel, there is discussion of the rape of an underage girl. There is also one scene where a character experiences unwanted kissing and touching. If you think this might be harmful or triggering to you, please feel free to give this book a pass. Or if you'd like to know what page numbers to skip or want to contact me for more details, please visit my website at carriepack.com.

1 https://www.rainn.org/statistics/victims-sexual-violence

CHAPTER 1

Heather's got her stupid flannel shirt tied around her stupid, tiny waist. I don't know if I'm more annoyed that she looks cuter like that than I do or if it's because I know she's only wearing it as a fashion statement. She's no more into grunge music than I am into Ace of Base. It's been like this all year. Heather and her cronies walking around pretending to give a shit about music and social causes. In reality, they only care about that stuff so they can meet boys and go shopping.

We used to be best friends. We used to do everything together: We played softball in middle school, rode bikes around the neighborhood, went camping with our Brownie troop. Everything. Then Heather's mom bought her some lipstick and a bra, and it was like I didn't exist. She started hanging out with Adina Monroe, Jen Radford and Molly Zawicky, whose mothers also bought them makeup and adult underwear, and left me sitting at the bus stop with my Dr. Pepper Lip Smackers and my Discman.

In a weird sort of way, I guess I have her to thank for my flawless taste in music and absolute disdain for all that is mainstream, but sometimes—although I would never admit it to her—sometimes, I miss my best friend.

"Oh look, it's Flabby Tabby." Heather tosses her freshly dyed blonde hair over her shoulder and giggles. Her friends all follow suit. Molly oinks.

And sometimes I want to punch her in the face.

I duck my head and pretend not to hear her as I forge my way toward first period trigonometry. Sure, I'm fat, whatever. That doesn't bother me nearly as much as the nonstop judgment I get for it. Heather knows it bothers me; that's why she does it so I can hear. I still don't understand why she turned on me. Most days I don't care. I just keep my head down and ignore her, but some days it's tougher than others—especially on the days I'm an alien life-form walking alongside perfect specimens of the human race.

I'm starting to think this is just how life will be: fat and friendless. My only friend nowadays is Mike Bernbaum. And I use the term "friend" loosely. He's more like my music dealer. We swap CDs and the occasional cigarette behind the 7-Eleven. He works at the video store, and the only reason I talk to him at all is because he's *not* a girl.

As I edge my way past a cheerleader, a cloud of perfume assaults my nose and I hold my breath to keep from inhaling any more of it than I absolutely have to. The cheerleader's blocking the doorway to my classroom so she can passionately make out with her boyfriend for a few minutes before they're separated for a whole stupid hour. I mutter, "Excuse me," but they don't move.

I rub against the cheerleader as I pass. It's an accident, but she doesn't seem to think so.

"Watch it, fatso!" she says with a sneer. "That lesbo grabbed my ass," she says to her boyfriend.

"I can't blame her, babe." The boyfriend takes a squeeze for himself. She giggles, and he goes back to eating her face.

It's not a new thing, me getting called a lesbian. I confessed to Heather once that I thought Winona Ryder was cute, and now she tells everyone I'm gay. Some kid in my Spanish class asked me if he could watch me make out with another girl, so I'm pretty sure the whole school heard Heather's rumor. Truth is, I'm not sure if I'm gay or not. But I wish she'd shut her stupid mouth.

"Sorry," I mumble as I roll my eyes and snake my way through the rows of desks to find my seat near the front. It's easier to concentrate up here, and I don't have to serve as go-between for everyone passing notes. The teacher, Mrs. Sansone, is writing problems on the board.

"Hey, Tabitha," she says with a smile. "I swear one day you're going to get here earlier than me."

I smile. Why not? Mrs. Sansone is nice enough. Sure, her breath always smells of stale cigarettes and gallons of black coffee, but she's good at explaining complex equations and she never makes us do problems at the board. I like her. And she likes me because I answer questions when no one else will. Teachers generally like me because I'm quiet and get my work done on time.

The classroom slowly fills up and then the bell rings. Mrs. Sansone is still writing a problem on the board when Brad Mason slams his backpack onto his desk and kicks the back of my chair. I don't bother saying anything. If I do, he'll just kick harder. Asshole.

THE REST OF THE DAY is just as bad. I manage to drop my lunch—bland, freezer-burned cafeteria pizza—in my lap, leaving a nice blobby dark stain across my thighs. I can still smell the fake cheese and tasteless marinara in seventh period. I hear Heather giggling. I think Molly says something about me being "flabby *and* sloppy," but I do my best to ignore them by sitting on the other side of the classroom. By the time I meet up with Mike behind the 7-Eleven after school, I'm pissed off, sweaty, and, in true Tabitha Denton fashion, my eyeliner has migrated from my eyelids to just above my cheekbones. I don't know why I bother.

Mike must see on my face that I'm in no mood for small talk. He hands me an already-lit cigarette and nods once. I inhale deeply while trying not to cough. I hate smoking. I don't know why I do it, other than it gives me something to do with my hands. And I only do it when I hang out with Mike.

He's taller than me, but only because he's standing on the curb. It probably bothers him that we're the same height; I'm not really a fan either. If I have to be bigger horizontally, I'd rather be smaller vertically. Looking up at him, I wonder if he has a former friend who turned on him, too. I don't remember him from middle school. One day he was just *there*, wearing a faded Stüssy shirt and jeans that were made of more holes than denim.

He's wearing that same shirt today, but his jeans have been swapped for a newer pair. His nearly black hair obscures his eyes as he wraps his full lips around his cigarette. He hums to himself while he finishes his cigarette and lights another. He finally speaks.

"You interested in going to a concert with me on Saturday?"

I quirk an eyebrow. "Maybe. Who's playing?"

"A couple of local punk bands and that girl band you like, Bikini Kill."

"Yeah, sounds cool."

I try to hide my excitement to save face, but I've been dying to go to a Bikini Kill show since I found a dog-eared copy of a zine plastered with song lyrics and feminist rants in varying degrees of poor grammar. The writing was a rambling miasma of personal manifesto, crazed fangirl doodles and important social commentary that made me both want to edit it for them and write my own angry punk music. I take another drag and exhale slowly, savoring the tiny puff of white as it curls around my face and dissipates.

Mike hops down from the curb and kicks the toe of my boot. "Those new?" he asks.

"New to me. I got them from a thrift store. I'm pretty sure they were someone's work boots." I bang the toe of my left boot against the side of the building as hard I as I can.

"Steel toe. Nice." Mike's words are decorated with smoke as the acrid smell floats between us.

The boots look awesome, but my feet are sweating, and I'm sure they'll reek when I take them off. Doesn't matter. It's a statement. A statement that maybe got me an invite to a Bikini Kill show.

"I didn't know you liked girl bands." I'm digging but I'm trying to get a read on Mike. We don't usually talk too much, and that's the way I like it. But today, there's something he's not telling me.

"I'm into whatever," he says with an air of fake nonchalance.

Of course, I only know it's fake because I saw him pull the same move on a girl he liked last year. Mike always says, "He who cares least has the least to lose." So he's trying to show me he cares less than I do? Okay. Two can play that game—even if his dark eyes are pulling me in. Did he always have those dimples?

"Yeah well, maybe I can go. I'll have to see." I scuff the heel of my boot on the bright yellow curb at the head of the parking space we're standing in. It leaves a satisfying black streak on the painted concrete.

Mike and I finish our cigarettes, and he says he'll try to call me about the concert. He throws in a few "whatevers" to sound bored, and I pretend not to notice.

I take my time getting home.

My house is on a tree-lined street in a neighborhood of older homes. The shag carpet and linoleum sport putrid shades of brown, orange and green that haven't been in style since the Nixon administration. I'm not sure they were in style then. Who would *ever* want their house to look like someone vomited pea soup everywhere? My parents, apparently.

As I hit the edge of our cul-de-sac, I pass Mrs. Zimmerman. She's the lone retiree on our street and spends every afternoon either in her garden or reading on her front porch. Today she's kneeling over her spring annuals and pulling up weeds.

"Hi, Mrs. Z!" For her benefit, I force my natural scowl into the hint of a smile.

She looks up and smiles at me from under her large sun hat. Her skin has the look of broken-in leather, so she only recently must have discovered the joys of UV protection. "Hello, Tabitha. Where's your boyfriend?"

I resist rolling my eyes and choose to shrug instead. In Mrs. Zimmerman's world, every girl gets a boyfriend.

"Ah, don't worry," she says. "A pretty thing like you? You'll be beating them off with a stick before long."

God, I hope not. I'd prefer to stay invisible, thank you very much. But I don't say this. I smile at Mrs. Zimmerman and continue toward my house.

There aren't any cars in the driveways on our cul-de-sac. Everyone's still at work, but by six, the street will be swarming with four-door sedans, minivans and station wagons. Lots of working parents where I live. Tons. Heaps. A plethora. It seems like my parents are the only ones divorced, though. Of course, Heather's perfect parents still hold hands in public. Barf.

Our house isn't anything special—small with no frills—but I've always liked it better than Heather's house. Her house is positively cavernous with its big, sweeping staircase and five bedrooms. When we were kids, she was always over at my place, though. She said our house was cozier. Whatever. I would have killed for her bedroom with the window seat and canopy bed. Doesn't matter now, though. One more thing to add to the "Reasons I hate Heather Davidson" list. It's a long list.

My key sticks in the latch, so I have to jiggle the handle to get the tumbler to engage. Sparky, our ten-year-old mutt with a spot-on impression of a dirty mop, barks from inside.

"Shut up, you dumb dog!"

Sparky barks louder as I stumble through the door. Then, with his dog genius, he realizes it's me and jumps up to lick my face.

"Ugh! Get off!"

Sparky sulks into the corner and flops down. We both know he'll find his way into my bed tonight, and I'll wake up tomorrow with a face full of fur.

"Dumb dog," I mutter.

I dump my backpack in the foyer and grab a bag of chips from the kitchen to go with my usual Dr. Pepper. Then I go upstairs to get my homework out of the way.

The phone rings before I even rip the potato chip bag open.

"Hey," Mike's voice drawls over the line. He always sounds like he's high, but I don't think I've ever seen him smoke anything other than his usual menthols. He's simply that laid back, or at least he's trying to be. His immediate phone call says otherwise. "We can pay the cover at the door for ten bucks, but if you can get a fake ID, it's only five."

"I've got the ten," I say, not wanting Mike to know I tried to get a fake ID once. It cost me fifty dollars for a faded picture of an Indian guy named Mark Chaudhary, who was very obviously *not* me. It's in my bottom desk drawer under some old coloring books. It will never see the light of day.

"Cool," he says. "I'll meet you behind the store at nine-thirty. Bring the boots." The wink in his voice makes me cringe.

"Okay." When did we start doing the flirty thing? I didn't sign up for this.

"See you Saturday," he says, and the line goes dead.

I spend the rest of the afternoon wrestling with an essay for English and errant, interrupting wonderings: "Is this a date?" and "Do I want it to be a date?"

Eventually I give up on both and fall asleep in my clothes. I never hear my mom come in.

The club is dirty and small, and I have to stand on my tiptoes to see the stage, but I don't care because these are my people: the hardscrabble freaks and losers who are angry at the world for their lot in life. Dramatic? Sure. But no one here looks at me like I'm some sort of zoo animal. An elephant with too much hair. A rhinoceros missing her horn. Here I am just a girl with cool boots, who maybe looks like she could kick your ass.

Mike seems in his element, too, and taller somehow, protective almost. When a guy with a safety pin through his left eyebrow bumps into me during the opening act, Mike shoves him back. At first I think we've won, but Eyebrow Piercing continues to thrash. I step to the side and let him go crazy. Who cares? This band is shit anyway. Mike lifts his brow as if to say, "Want me to kick his ass?" But I shake my head. No point in getting kicked out before the good bands start. We make our way to the other side of the venue where I can see the stage a little better.

We stand there for a while, taking in the scene. The opening band continues to suck. I'm not even sure the bass player's amp is on. Their sound is top-heavy, like a car stereo with the speakers blown out. Mike nods in the direction of the merch tables. Looks like all the bands are selling tapes and a couple of girls are handing out flyers. We sidestep the thrashing masses to get a better look. I pass up the tapes; I don't get my allowance until Monday, and I already blew my savings on the boots. A girl about my age catches my eye and smiles. Her brown hair is barely past shoulder length and much shinier than mine. Bright pink barrettes frame her pale face near her forehead. It should make her look childish, but instead she looks cool. I smile back.

"Hey, you interested in doing some shit?" she asks. Her pale green eyes sparkle with determination.

"Like what?"

"About all the bullshit in the world that girls have to put up with."

Thinking she's joking, I laugh. "That's ambitious."

"Just because we're girls doesn't mean we can't change things. Here." She hands me the flyer I'd noticed her passing out. "We meet on Tuesdays."

"Thanks." Before I get a chance to read it, she thrusts another piece of paper under my nose.

"This is our zine," she says. "It's just some thoughts and stuff, but it's free. If you want to subscribe, send a dollar and some postage to that address on the back."

I flip over the tiny booklet—it's photocopied and folded to look like a small magazine. The pages are a mixture of typed and hand-written passages with pictures that seem to be cut out of *Sassy* or *Seventeen*. It reminds me of that Bikini Kill zine I had.

In the absence of anything better to say, I mumble, "Cool," and shove the zine into my pocket along with the flyer. The girl smiles again, and my stomach flutters, just as Mike taps me on the shoulder.

"They're getting set up. Let's try to get a spot closer to the stage."

"Sure." I turn to the brunette, wave and offer a halfhearted "Thanks." I still don't know what the hell she gave me, but I wish I could talk to her longer.

While the band sets up, a petite Asian girl stands up at the mic and shouts, "All the girls, come to the front!" I hesitate. Maybe she's talking to her friends. I glance around for a clue. No one seems to be moving. Mike nudges me, and I stumble over my heavy boots.

"Girls to the front!" she shouts again. "Come on. All the girls need to be up here, right down front where the band can see you." She waves her arms wildly, beckoning us forward. A few girls follow her command, but I'm frozen.

"Tabitha, you're a girl," Mike insists, shouting over the noise.

I inch closer, but I still feel like a fraud. I'm not cool enough to be part of this group of girls.

"*All* girls to the front!" the girl onstage shouts again, and the room reverberates with feedback.

I'm attempting some half-assed excuse when a pale girl with hair so red it could only have come from a bottle grabs me by the elbow. Without a word, she tugs hard on my left arm. Before I know it, I'm close enough to the stage that I can reach out and touch it, and the redhead still has her arm looped through mine. I want to pull away but I don't. She smells like vanilla body spray, and her arm feels like silk where it grazes my bare skin. We're in this together now.

The house lights dim, and the crowd erupts into screams as the band rips into their first song. By the chord change, I've forgotten all about my awkwardness and I dance my fucking face off.

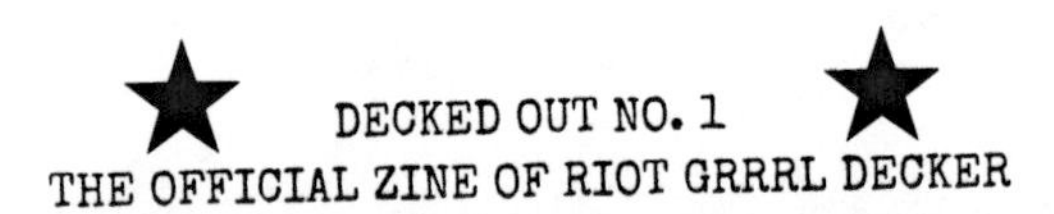
DECKED OUT NO. 1
THE OFFICIAL ZINE OF RIOT GRRRL DECKER

MY ZINE IS BETTER THAN YOUR SCENE

So at the Lipstick Revolver show last month I met this rad chick named Marty who told me about this group called Riot Grrrl (if you've ever heard of Bikini Kill or Heavens to Betsy you know what we're talking about) and we decided to start our own group right here in Decker. For now, we're meeting in Marty's basement; it's not as bad as it sounds, promise. She has a pool table and comfy furniture. We just need to bring our own pop and stuff so her mom doesn't go nuts. This is gonna be an all-ages thing, so bring your little sisters, girlfriends, cousins, bffs, whatever. Riot GRRRL is all about DOING STUFF. We want to be heard and we're sick as f*ck with being left out of the punk and grunge scene because we're chicks. We are sick of walking to our front doors at night with our keys between our fingers so we can gouge out the eyes of our rapists. We're sick of being called fat because we don't look like supermodels. We're sick of being called whores because we dare to wear midriff tops. We're sick and tired of being sick and tired.

We want to change that. We want people to take us seriously and we want to support each other with some girl power! This is a girls revolution! JOIN OUR GRRRL GANG!!!!!!!!

Now our meetings won't all be super serious. We're hoping to just chill too and some of us want to start a band. Marty and I were brainstorming names the other day and came up with some cool ones. Check it out and let us know if you use one so we don't overlap.

This is gonna be killer. See you... oh, I guess I should say when the meetings are. We plan to meet Tuesdays at 6 at Marty's—it's the address on the back of the zine.

xoxo,
Kate

BAND NAMES FOR BADASS GIRL GROUPS

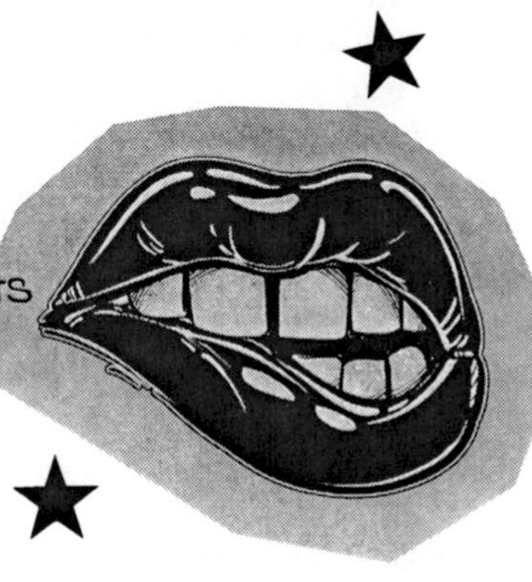

Battle Bots
Bottled Blondes
June Meat Cleavers
The Menstrual Cyclists
Vagina Slims
Tits and Slash
Tits and Gash
The Pain Austens

HARD ROCK

Toxic Shock
Dandelion Queef
Suicidal Butterflies
9021-Ho
Lace Panties
The Rags

Brandon Walsh's Virginity
Menstrual Weekend
Menstrual Oyster
Twat's Up Doc?
My Left Tit
Silicone Breast Implants
Toe Pick
The Claires
Pubic Menace

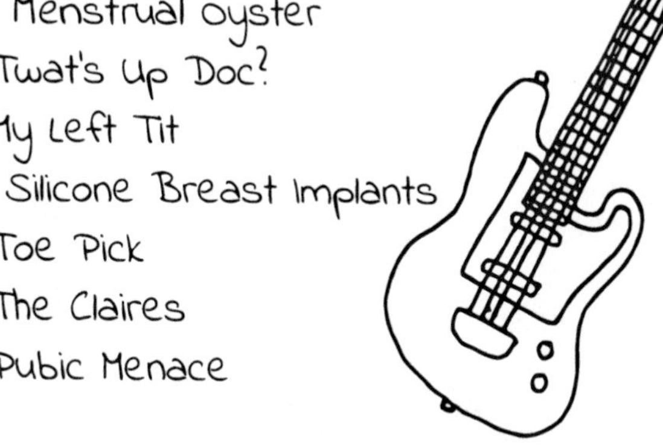

YESTERDAY BY KATE G.

Yesterday, my dad told me I had mosquito bites instead of boobs;
Yesterday, I saw an ad for a Wonderbra;
Yesterday, I realized my own father had sexualized me;
Yesterday, I bought a magazine that promised me "7 ways to wow him in bed!";
Yesterday, I learned I'm a commodity—made for male consumption;
Yesterday, a boy called me ugly, and I believed him;
Yesterday, I knew I'd never measure up;
Yesterday, I traded my soccer cleats for high heels;
Yesterday, I wondered if there is a way out;
Yesterday, I kissed a girl;
Yesterday, I got called a dyke;
Yesterday, I died a little inside;
Yesterday was my birthday.

A teenage feminist MANIFESTO by Marty DeVane

We are the generation who can change this shit. Misogyny. Patriarchy. Sexism. We need to wake up. Stop buying the push-up bras and pantyhose and going on crash diets. I want to spit in the face of consumerism and piss on the patriarchy. I want to wear frilly dresses and play in the mud. I want to punch things and dance ballet and eat an entire cake. I want to not care if my thighs touch. If I decide tomorrow that I don't want to shave my legs or my pits, then I won't. If I want to wear red lipstick, I will.

★ I am a woman.

★ I am a human.

★ I am.

CHAPTER 2

I SKIP THE RIOT GRRRL meeting that first Tuesday after the concert. I'm not sure why. Even after the concert, I'm left with a feeling of inadequacy. Guess you can't erase sixteen years of insecurity with one night of thrashing at a Bikini Kill show.

Instead I moon over that stupid flyer. I carry it everywhere and read it whenever I need a boost. The words "Smash the Patriarchy" printed in bold, block letters have become my internal mantra.

When Brad Mason catches me reading the flyer in first period, he laughs. "Don't tell me you're thinking of joining those whiny-ass bitches."

I glare at him over my shoulder. *Smash the Patriarchy!*

Brad sneers. "They're all just a bunch of man-hating, hairy-armpitted lesbians."

"Shut up." I turn around in my seat and try to ignore him.

"Are you a lesbian, Tabitha?" He smirks.

"That's none of your business." I crumple the flyer and shove it in my pocket. Even though I have no intention of using it, I keep my hand tightly balled in a fist. Tears sting my eyelids, but I refuse to let them fall. I might be a chicken, but I've got standards. No crying in public. Not after the last time.

Brad's gaze burns through my back the entire hour, but I don't spill a single tear. Not one. *Smash the Patriarchy!*

EVERY DAY THAT WEEK, IN first period, I smooth out the flyer and read it again. Only this time I'm more careful about letting anyone see it. I eventually chicken out and wad it up, shoving it into the deepest, darkest crevice of my backpack. Later, usually in last period, I dig it out and smooth it as best I can, pondering the twelve words of text I soon have memorized. I even have Marty's address stored in the depths of my brain. She only lives about six blocks from me. How great would it be to meet some girls who liked the same stuff that I do? Who have gone through the same stuff? Who aren't Heather Davidson and her bitchy sycophants?

I glance in Heather's direction and notice she's wearing the silver hoop earrings I got her for her birthday last year. It was the last time I hung out with her before she completely disowned me. Although, if I'm honest, she'd written me off long before then. Loyalty was the only thing keeping us connected at all and even that couldn't trump popularity—not with boyfriends and makeup and parties on the line. For her fifteenth birthday, Heather had a pool party and invited all the cool girls from our class. She told me she had a secret plan to get us in with their crowd, and I was so excited. Then Jen Radford, in all her tactful coolness, asked her why she had invited the fat girl. Of course, we both knew Jen meant me. I was *the* fat girl. I remember looking around at the other girls, all skinny and tan in their bikinis, and me in a navy-blue one-piece covered with a *Ren & Stimpy* T-shirt. To drive her point home, Jen shoved me in the pool and joked that everyone could go whale watching now. And Heather laughed. She was probably still laughing when I walked through my front door twenty minutes later, sopping wet and minus a best friend.

By this time, I've been staring too long. Heather looks up and glares at me and then whispers something to Molly, who's taken my place at Heather's side. They're always together and always laughing about something. They erupt into a fit of giggles that I know is at my expense. Heather may be dead to me, but it still hurts. When I look at her I still see the little girl who told me she was going to marry Kirk Cameron and have twenty babies. Only now that girl has been consumed by a lip gloss-wearing harpy whose only mission in life is to make me miserable. I wish she'd go back to daydreaming about Kirk and his twenty brats and leave me the hell alone.

I force my attention back on the chapter we're supposed to be reading, but I can still feel their eyes on me. I try my best to care less than they do, but the hurt still niggles at the back of my mind, even as I try to read *Great Expectations*. I hate Dickens almost as much as I hate Heather, so it's easy to get distracted. My brain runs through every worry it can drum up. *What if the girls at this meeting are just like Heather and Jen and Molly? What if I'm the fat outcast who's the butt of all the jokes? What if no one likes me? What if Heather got to them first?* I'm not sure I could handle that again.

I crumple the flyer and shove it in my pocket. The ink is starting to wear off.

I try to smash down thoughts of the Chick Clique—yes, they actually call themselves that, and it makes me want to barf—as they continue to look my way and laugh. I blink to keep the tears from spilling. My vision is too blurry to copy the homework assignment, but I refuse to let Heather—or anyone else—see me cry.

When the bell rings, I toss the flyer in the trash.

"I DON'T KNOW WHY YOU let those jerks get to you," Mike says. He stubs out his cigarette and lights another one. "They are nasty, self-absorbed little girls. You don't need Heather Davidson in your life."

I like that Mike never calls girls bitches, even girls like Heather who deserve it. He says his mom doesn't like it when he demeans women. He gets in more trouble for saying "bitch" than he does for the f-word.

"I know you're right, but it gets under my skin. And she knows it." I pretend to squint into the sun so he can't see my traitorous tears.

He bumps his shoulder against mine. "So stop *letting* it get under your skin. Prove her wrong."

"Easier said than done, my friend." The closeness overwhelms me, so I take a couple of steps to kick an empty pop can. It goes skittering across the parking lot before coming to a stop in a puddle of greasy, brown water. I can relate. I'm more like that faded old can than other girls my age. "Why are girls such shits?"

"I don't think all girls are like that," Mike says. "You're not like that."

He pushes off the wall he's leaning on and steps closer as he tosses his cigarette in the same puddle. His brown eyes lock on mine, and my heart beats faster.

"I'm not?" The words sound hollow, but I can't think of anything else to say. It seems like more than we've said to each other in a month.

Pursing his full lips, Mike shakes his head. Holding my gaze, he tucks my hair behind my ear and then glances down to my lips and back up to my eyes. I think he might kiss me. Instead, he turns his head and spits. His saliva puddles and disappears into the pavement, and I'm grateful it didn't end up in my mouth.

"I gotta go. My mom wants me to help with dinner." It's an outright lie, but I don't want to stay here with Mike any longer. Something has changed between us, and I need time to process it.

"See you tomorrow," he says. It sounds like a question instead of a statement.

Unable to trust my own voice, I nod. I can feel Mike's gaze on my back as I walk away. I keep my posture as firm as I can, and I try to walk as if it's just another day, as if the ground beneath me hasn't shifted. But everything is different. I'm sure he can see it in my stride.

I need new friends.

THAT ALMOST-KISS OVERRIDES MY FEAR of rejection and pushes me into action. Plus, I have the address memorized, so I can't use throwing out the flyer as an excuse.

Marty's house looks a bit like mine, but it's much bigger—the longer I stare, the more it reminds me of Heather's house, especially the way the driveway wraps around in a half circle. I stand in that driveway staring at the front door until my feet begin to ache. I'm about to make my getaway when a car pulls up. It's a gold hatchback, and even with the windows up I can hear the music blaring. The white girl from the concert who gave me the flyer is driving; the Asian girl who was up onstage is in the passenger seat. When the driver sees me, she waves.

Shit. I've been spotted. No turning back now.

I hold up my hand in a halfhearted greeting and try to smile, but I suddenly feel extremely awkward and out of place. These girls are much cooler than I am. The driver has perfectly lined eyes and a button nose. Her shoulder-length brown hair is shampoo-ad shiny, but now, instead of wearing the baby barrettes, she's pulled it back into a cute ponytail. My ponytail always manages to look lazy. I tug on my hair, hoping to smooth some of the frizz.

As the other girl exits the car, her black hair, sculpted into a perfect angled bob, falls beautifully across her face. And her petite, perfectly proportioned frame is evident even beneath her oversized babydoll dress. Meanwhile, my stomach strains against my waistband, so, hoping to look smaller, I suck it in. My heart races as I try to decide the best route to cut and run. They'll probably think I'm a fat freak with my pale skin, boring gray eyes and mousy brown hair.

"Hey," the driver says. She sounds almost happy to see me. "Didn't I see you at the Bikini Kill show last week?"

"Yeah, um, you gave me the flyer." My voice squeaks. Actually squeaks! What am I, a mouse?

"Cool." She smiles again. "I'm Kate Goldberg and this is Cherie Wong."

"We're so glad you came!" Cherie gushes. She looks far less aggressive than she did at the concert. Of course, she's not screaming into a microphone, so that might have something to do with it. Her smile is welcoming and real.

I'm not sure what to say, so I attempt another smile. I bet it looks as awkward as I feel. "I'm Tabitha," I say. "I'm not sure I'm supposed to be here. I just..." I don't know how to finish that sentence.

"Oh, we all feel that way at first," Kate says, putting her arm around me as if she's known me for years. "Don't worry. Everyone is going to love you, if your taste in music is anything to go by."

We're quiet while Kate rings the doorbell. A shout from inside insists we come in and head downstairs.

"Marty likes to make an entrance," Kate says, "but she's cool... in her own way. You'll see."

Cherie smiles. "Last week she dyed her hair bright blue, but it faded to a half-assed green. I wonder what color it will be this week." She winks at me and leads the way into the house.

I laugh, but I wish I had the guts to dye my hair a crazy color.

"Tabitha, hmm? Your mom think she's a witch or something?"

"Obsessed with *Bewitched*, actually. Apparently she watched a lot of reruns while she was pregnant with me. So you're not far off."

"Still, it's a pretty name."

"Thanks," I mutter. It's the first time someone my age has complimented my name instead of making fun of it. No condescending fingers on the nose, attempting to mimic the childlike wiggle from the TV show. No shouts of "Flabby Tabby" as I try not to cry. I don't know what to do with that.

"So, how old are you, Tabitha? Still in high school?" Kate flips on the light at the top of the stairs and descends.

"Yeah, I go to North Decker. I'm a sophomore."

"Sixteen?" Cherie asks.

I nod.

"I went to N-Deck," Kate says. "Mrs. Sansone still there?"

"Yep, I have her for trig."

"She was great. The only teacher I ever had who made math bearable."

"I hate math," Cherie says. "When you've got a Chinese last name, teachers always expect you to be good at it, but I'm not. Maybe if I had a teacher like that."

"Cherie went to Central. We're at the community college together."

Our conversation is interrupted when we hear footsteps on the stairs and Cherie asks me to help set out chairs. Marty, who has bright pink hair today, barks orders that Kate and Cherie ignore in favor of doing their own thing. I introduce myself, and, after a brief moment of excitement at my presence, Marty gives me orders, too. My eyes follow her as we set up. She's bigger than the other girls, but not as fat as me. She moves like she either doesn't notice or doesn't care. Guessing by her snug-fitting shirt and shorts, it's probably the latter. I envy her.

The room gradually fills up with girls—some are as young as fourteen, but most of them are friends of Kate, Cherie and Marty, so they're a bit older than I am. Everyone seems to get along, and no one seems to be left out, which kind of blows my mind. I didn't know that was possible. Everyone has someone to sit with, and they all introduce themselves to me. One is a girl who goes to my school; she's a senior named Jenny whom I've seen in the halls but have never spoken to. She smiles at me as if we're old friends.

"Hey, I think we have gym together," she says. "Well, the same period. It's Tabitha, right?"

I nod. It's the only communication I can manage. How does this girl—a real-life popular senior!—know my name? I'm invisible.

While I'm still trying to reconcile my own image of myself with the way Jenny smiles at me, Kate motions for me to sit by her. It's surreal to walk into a room and be welcomed. My chest clenches, and I try to take deep breaths.

"Hey, everybody," Marty says, once the group is quiet and formed into a lopsided circle. "I'm Martina DeVane, but everyone usually calls me Marty. I wanted to start off today's meeting with a question. What was the moment this week that you were treated like a commodity? For me it was when I went to buy this hair dye and the woman at the register said I wouldn't be able to catch a boyfriend with fuchsia hair." Marty rolls her eyes and I hear Kate mutter something like, "bitch." Marty continues, "So I told her to suck my left one."

Applause breaks out and Marty sticks out her tongue in a way I've only seen punk rockers do. This girl is so crazy and fierce. I love it. Kate and Cherie made me feel welcome, but Marty makes me want to take on the world. She's gritty and edgy and takes no shit. Every other word out of her mouth is a four-letter one. In fact, the first thing she said to me was, "Fuck yeah! A new recruit."

The next girl is a fifteen-year-old from Central who says her brother called her "unfuckable." The one after that says her aunt pointed out her unshaven legs at a family party and everyone, including her own mother, laughed at her. And so it goes: story after story of girls being degraded or sexualized without their consent. When it's my turn, I hesitate. I have nothing as heart-wrenching as these girls.

"It's okay," Kate says. She puts her hand on my back and rubs small circles. That makes me brave.

I take a deep breath and confess, "My story's nowhere near as bad as that, but I guess I felt like that when my former best friend called me Flabby Tabby and made fun of me." Embarrassed, I hang my head and wait for the next girl to speak.

"Not as bad?" Marty interrupts. "That's almost worse. Girls should stick up for each other."

A couple of girls shout "Yeah," and I lift my head to find Kate smiling at me. Maybe Mike was right. Maybe this group will be different. I'll reserve judgment, at least until the next meeting.

After everyone has answered the question, the rest of the meeting is more or less an informal party. Girls take turns bringing up stuff they want to talk about, but mostly we talk in small groups. Toward the end, Marty breaks out a guitar and plays a melancholy tune while Cherie sings along. When she gets to the chorus, a bunch of girls sing along.

"Fuck the man;
fuck my uncle;
fuck it all, my friend.
We are women who won't be silenced,
never again the end."

Applause breaks out, and a few girls hug. One of the youngest has tears streaming down her plump cheeks. Kate hugs her, and the girl collapses in her arms. The room is silent until the girl finally lifts her head to speak.

"I'm sorry," she says, sniffing.

"Don't be sorry, Becky," Kate says. "What that guy did to you is shitty." She strokes Becky's hair.

"What happened to her?" I whisper to Cherie.

"Date rape," she says, her thin lips curled into an ugly sneer. "Well, 'date' is a loose term. It was a guy in her church youth group. They were at a retreat, and he slipped something into her pop. She woke up naked on a blanket in the woods. He claimed she had been begging for it."

"But she's so young," I say. My brain won't process it. I can't understand how a girl younger than me could be violated like that, and by someone she knows. "She's just a kid."

"Like that's gonna stop a shitbag rapist like Jason Hartley," Cherie says through gritted teeth. "We should plaster his name all over town."

"Well, at least he's in jail, right?"

Cherie scoffs. "Hardly. They sent him on a mission trip to Haiti. His parents said he needed to learn to stay away from 'girls like Becky.' They think the focus on others will help him to heal." She rolls her eyes. "Can you believe that? *He* needs to heal, like he's the one who can't go a day without breaking into tears. Like he's not the one who chose to drug a thirteen-year-old girl and undress her and violate her."

"But it's not her fault," I say, suddenly angry at this guy I've never met—and his stupid parents. "Why would his parents...? That doesn't make any sense."

"No, it fucking doesn't." Marty's voice comes from behind me. "But sadly, most of us have stories like that."

I glance around the room; my eyes dart from one girl to the next. They all look so normal. How are they still sane? How have I escaped this horror?

"Oh, don't be so dramatic, Marty." Cherie shoves her shoulder. "Some of us haven't been raped. You're scaring her."

"It's rape whenever a man violates us," she says. "Even if it's verbally. You heard what some of these girls said today." She levels her gaze at me. "You've been called fat. But what about a whore? A bitch? Maybe even a lesbian, like that's some sort of insult."

I nod, blinking to keep the tears from forming. Me and my stupid tears.

"That's fucking rape. Every time someone degrades us, or tells us what to look like or how to feel or what to do, they are violating us."

"Stop comparing rape and misogyny," Kate says, sounding exasperated. "Sexism is brutal and it needs to stop, but it's not the same as what happened to Becky. I'd gladly take being called a bitch a million times if it meant stopping all the rapes in the world."

"But that's my point. You shouldn't have to be subjected to either! When men call us bitches, it degrades us and makes it okay for them to rape us." As she gets more impassioned, Marty's round face begins to match her hair.

Kate rolls her eyes. This is obviously an argument they've had before. "Whatever, Marty. I just think you should tone it down a bit. That's all."

"Don't fucking tell me what to do in my own house!"

Kate shakes her head and gives me an apologetic smile. "I think I'm going to go before this gets any more heated. Would you like a ride home, Tabitha? Cherie and I could drop you off."

"That would be great, thanks." As much as I'm fascinated by Marty, I'll gladly accept the ride to get away from the terror that is her rage. I thank her for hosting the meeting.

"You're coming back, right?" Marty's dark eyes burn through me as she grabs my arm. "I swear I'm not always like this."

"Oh, yes, she is," Cherie says. She sticks out her tongue to show she's teasing, but Marty glares at her anyway.

"I'm just passionate about stuff," Marty explains with a smile. "Can't fault a girl for that, right?"

I smile. "No, I think it's good to care."

"See? I knew she was cool," Marty says.

My heart soars. Marty thinks I'm cool. I'm incredulous; my mouth breaks into a wide grin.

"Hey, look!" Marty says. "Tabitha has teeth after all." She laughs, and I know she's teasing me because she likes me. I like not feeling shoved aside.

"See you next week!" shouts a girl whose name I forgot.

"Bye!" yells another.

As I follow Kate and Cherie up the stairs, my boots seem lighter even with the steel covering my toes. Or maybe it's my mood. The black cloud that has followed me for months thins and the first rays of sunlight poke through.

CHAPTER 3

School, as usual, knocks me off my cloud, and the hazy miserable fog returns… literally. The day starts with a torrential downpour that soaks everything from my hair to my socks, including a meticulously written essay for English lit. The ink has bled all over, and only a few words are legible. As I frantically try to rewrite it in first period—struggling to remember the quotes I used and the arguments I made—I notice an overpowering wet dog smell. It overwhelms my nose and makes it hard to concentrate. Some other kids seem to notice it too; whispers travel around the room in waves.

Brad slams his backpack onto his desk behind me and sniffs loudly. "Whoa, Tabitha, you reek."

I sniff harder. It can't be me. I am soaked to the skin, like I just went swimming, and anyway, I showered this morning.

"It's not me, you cretin."

Brad looks confused. I'm proud of myself for using a word that seems to have baffled him, even momentarily, but Amber, the girl sitting next to me, leans over and inhales.

"I think it *is* you," she says, her face scrunching up in a grimace as she bends and sniffs again. "Ew. It's those nasty old boots." She pinches her nose and waves her other hand in front of her face.

I bend over to get closer to my feet, and sure enough, the smell is radiating off my boots. It reminds me of that time my mom forgot a bag of groceries in the car, and we couldn't get rid of the rotting chicken smell for weeks.

My face burns as I try to figure out how to get rid of the odor. I can't go barefoot; I'll get detention. I could wear my gym shoes, but they're on the other side of the school in my locker. I'd never make it there and back before the bell rings. I'm going to have to sit through all of first period smelling like the Swamp Thing. I shift in my seat and try to tuck my feet under my desk but the smell seems to be getting stronger.

"Mrs. Sansone," Amber says, raising her hand. "Tabitha's boots are rank. Can I switch seats?"

"Thanks a lot, traitor," I mumble.

Mrs. Sansone glances at me and then my boots. She offers a sympathetic smile through her grimace. "Tabitha, do you need to go change? I can give you a hall pass."

I've never been more grateful to be a teacher's favorite. I try to shrink as I walk to her desk to get the pass, but I've never felt more enormous and obvious. My face flushes as I notice more students covering their noses as I walk by. Shame has a smell, and it's wet thrift store boots.

The hallways are quiet and eerie without students. I like it; it's more peaceful, and less like a minefield of awkwardness waiting to happen. In the cavernous space, the smell from my boots dissipates. It has somewhere to go besides up the nostrils of my classmates.

As if they're trying to remind me of my mission, my boots squeak and squish on the tile as I make my way to the locker room. I won't have time to rewrite my English essay, but at least I won't smell like a dead animal soaked in armpit sweat.

The locker room is far less treacherous without clusters of girls in every corner—girls who are far less concerned with revealing skin than I am, who simply strip down to their bras and panties without a care, who don't have cellulite at sixteen or fat rolls so deep I could store snacks in them. No, blissfully empty, the rows of hunter-green lockers have lost their power to make me feel worthless. I straighten my spine and hold my head a little higher.

I stop short in front of my locker. Something is wrong. The lock looks odd; it's sideways in the latch and hanging open. Did I forget to lock it?

I rip open the door. My gym clothes are lying in a soggy mess on the bottom of my locker, and it's not from rain water. There's a sticky sweet smell reminiscent of grape cough syrup that's even stronger than the odor from my boots. Well, grape shoes are better than dead animal boots, I guess. I reach into the locker, trying to keep my hands from the worst of the puddle. The only problem is, my shoes are nowhere to be found. I hadn't noticed because of the wet clothes. There's a grape-soaked T-shirt and my shorts, but no shoes. They're gone.

Why the hell would someone steal my ratty old gym shoes?

When the shock wears off—and I've searched my now-empty locker again—I am overwhelmed with defeat. I can't go back to class. I'll have to sneak out and go home. I can go now while everyone is in class. I have a hall pass. No one would realize I was leaving until it was too late.

It would also give me a chance to take my gym clothes home to wash them. They're doing me no good in my locker soaked in… Is that grape soda?

I yank my lunch out of my backpack and dump the sandwich and chips in the trash. Then I shove my sticky gym clothes into the brown bag. It's a tight fit, but at least I won't have grape goo all over my books. I grab paper towels from the bathroom and clean out my locker as best I can. Then I double-check that it's actually locked. Not that it matters now; there's nothing in it.

Just as I'm about to leave, the locker room door swings open. First period gym must be getting out. I duck into a bathroom stall in case one of the coaches shows up and realizes I'm in the wrong place. I'll wait it out until the bell rings. I can sneak out between classes. No problem.

I didn't account for the second period class showing up to change. The noise in the locker room grows louder and louder, and then it gets quiet.

I sit on that stupid toilet for a good fifteen minutes until the warning bell rings. This is probably as empty as the locker room is going to get. I stand up, ready to make a break for it, when I hear familiar voices.

"She's so disgusting. I can't believe you used to be friends with her."

"Ugh. Don't remind me."

As usual, I have all the luck. It's Heather and Molly.

"Amber said she smelled like rotting meat." Molly's cruel laugh magnifies her disdain.

"Rotting meat *soaked in urine,*" Heather corrects. Her accompanying laugh is unfamiliar and cold. So much has changed; I realize I don't know her anymore. At all.

Hot, angry tears soak my cheeks as I try to remain silent and invisible. Confronting them would only make it worse, so I hold my breath and try to calm myself while I pray they leave soon.

Finally, the second period bell rings, and the locker room clears out. It takes me a few minutes to regain my composure, but when I do, I run for the exit.

My boots squish the entire way home.

I SHARE THE WHOLE STORY with the other Riot Grrrls the following Tuesday. All of them are sympathetic, several of them are visibly angry and even Jenny has a suggestion for getting the smell out of the boots: "Just wipe them down with diluted vinegar and then let them dry for a few days," she says.

"Next time don't wear them when it rains," a dark-haired girl says.

Thanks, Captain Obvious.

Overall, though, sharing my embarrassment is cathartic. Being able to bitch about it without fear of being judged is liberating. It seems like it's that way for a lot of us. Our Riot Grrrl meetings are special, a way to vent and feel a part of something while working toward a larger goal. Of course, that goal is amorphous and changeable. One day it's "sticking it to the man" and the next it's "saving girls from rapists." Some days it's both. Smash the patriarchy, right?

The meetings begin to blur, one into the next. We talk about our problems; we encourage each other and we become friends.

I get along with almost everyone—a new sensation for me; I'm used to being invisible and friendless—but I've become closest with Kate and Cherie. Even Marty seems to have accepted me as one of her flock. Riot Grrrl is my refuge from the festering wound that is my high school and the salve on the scar of my friendship with Heather.

I'm pretty sure she was the one who soaked my gym clothes in grape soda. I can't prove it, but she's the only one who knows how much I hate grape flavoring. I can't figure out why she'd do it. I've never done anything to her, and it's not a very high-profile prank. She's not even in my gym class to see me discover the mess. In the end, I decide it doesn't matter. The smell washes out, and the clothes aren't stained. But I take extra care locking my gym locker—double- and triple-checking it every day after I change.

It's only a couple of months before the end of the school year. I just need to make it a few more weeks. The community college gets out earlier, so I spend even more time with Kate, Cherie and Marty.

One Wednesday afternoon, we're all sitting on the floor in Marty's basement listening to a Heavens to Betsy tape Cherie brought. There are a few good songs, but I'm distracted. Kate is wearing a black ribbon as a choker and she smells like something fruity. I'm acutely aware of her presence, even without looking at her, and it makes the hairs on my arm stand on end. I try to keep my body contained in as little horizontal space as possible. I sit with my back uncomfortably straight and lean on the side of the couch, but we're sitting close to each other so we don't have to turn the stereo up. Marty's dad works nights, and, if we wake him up, there'll be hell to pay. Eventually my left leg falls asleep, and I have to adjust. I lean to one side and release my foot from under my thigh. My toes tingle with pinpricks as the circulation returns. As I flex and stretch, Kate's thigh grazes mine. It's completely accidental, but it thrills me nonetheless. I think I might actually explode. I'm suddenly very aware of my own breathing and how close Kate's hand is. I want to grab it, but I don't. I'm not gay. I have a thing for Mike. Or maybe he has a thing for me.

I try to focus on the lyrics of the song that's playing.

Eyes closed, Cherie taps along with the bass line. Marty is focused on a notebook in her lap and the stack of mail addressed to Riot Grrrl. When the song ends, Cherie gets up to turn the tape over. It's quiet, and then Kate drops a bomb on us.

"I think I might be into chicks," Kate says. Her expression is nonchalant despite the nuclear reaction she's just unleashed. In fact, she doesn't even look up from the issue of *Sassy* she's thumbing through. My face reddens. Can she read my thoughts?

"What?" My voice is hoarse, so I clear my throat. "Like, *like* them like them?"

"Yeah, why not?" she says with a shrug. "I mean look at Winona Ryder." She holds up the magazine and shows me a photo of the actress pouting. "Have you ever seen someone so brooding and… I don't know, cool?"

I think about it. Sure. Lots of girls are brooding and cool. And some of them are super cute too, like Winona. I've admired her before, and, of course, Heather made fun of me for it. But that doesn't mean I'm attracted to them. Does it?

I think of Mike and his dark eyes, his tan skin, his dimples and his lips pursed tightly around a cigarette. My stomach flutters. I look at Kate and it flips again. Maybe I'm getting sick.

"So what? Lots of people think Winona's cool," Marty says. "Doesn't mean we're all lesbians."

"I didn't say I was a lesbian," Kate says.

I look at her sideways, trying not to seem too obvious. I sit on my hands to keep them from shaking.

"Oh, so you're bi now?" Marty asks, her words soaked in disdain.

"So what if I am?" Kate retorts. "I don't have to fit into some neat little box for you, or anyone else."

That makes me smile. I like the thought of someone being attracted to more than one gender. It's tinted with infinite possibilities. Plus, Kate's confident in a way I can only dream of being, and that makes me oddly protective of her.

"I think it's cool if you're bi," I mumble. *Please let it be cool with everyone else*, I think.

Kate smiles at me and my stomach flips. "Thanks, Tab." She throws her arm around me and glares at Marty. My heart beats faster.

"Whatever." Marty shakes her head and goes back to the pile of letters our tiny Riot Grrrl chapter has received. Cherie pushes play, and Kate and I turn our attention back to the music. Cherie paints her toenails.

"Hell, yeah!" Marty shrieks. "We got a new place to meet, girls. Bigger, more visibility and most importantly, no nosy moms or sleeping dads."

"I thought you liked hosting," Cherie says. She blows on her now sparkly blue toenails.

"I'll still technically be hosting," Marty says with an air of self-imposed authority. "Just on a grander scale."

Kate rolls her eyes, and I laugh. Marty is so very Marty sometimes.

"Where is it?" I ask, hoping it's still within walking distance. My mom has failed yet again to come through on the car front and my bike's had a flat tire for over a year.

"The community rec center on Collins." Marty's face is buried in the letter. "Says we have to set up and take down—like we don't already—and organize a roadside trash pickup once a month."

"That's not so bad," Cherie says. "Beats the hell out of paying for a space like my church wanted."

"Exactly," Marty says. "Looks like we can start using it next month. Anyone want to go with me to check it out?" She stands up, places her hands on her hips and stares at me and Kate.

"Right now?" Kate asks.

"No time like the present."

Kate looks at me and back to Marty. "We wanted to finish listening to this tape, and Tabitha's got to be home in an hour."

Marty rolls her eyes. "Cherie?"

Cherie looks at her toes and the bottle of polish still in her hand. "I— Well, I guess I could if—"

Marty cuts her off. "Great. Let's go and leave these two to their… whatever. Just make sure you guys lock the door when you leave. My mom won't be home until six and she'll flip if the place isn't bolted down like Fort Knox."

Cherie reluctantly follows Marty upstairs, and I hear Marty whisper-shout, "I've got flip-flops, for fuck's sake, Cherie!"

Kate and I giggle, sharing a moment of camaraderie about our predictable friends. Marty gets so frustrated with Cherie's overt femininity; she insists makeup is profoundly anti-feminist and never misses an opportunity to tell us so.

Kate rewinds the tape. "I think we missed most of that song," she says.

I nod, and Kate returns to her spot on the floor next to me. She leaves the magazine open but doesn't continue reading it.

By the time the last haunting notes of "Paralyzed" fade out, I'm hyperaware of how close Kate and I are sitting. My heart races as I try not to move and burst our private bubble.

Kate reclines on the thick shag carpet and folds her hands behind her head. "God, I want to sing like that."

I lie down beside her and turn my head in her direction. "I bet you could." My voice is barely above a whisper; we're lying so close.

She waves me off. "Nah, I sing like a dying cat, but you're sweet for saying it." She gives me a sideways glance and a soft grin that sends shivers all the way down to my toes.

I focus my attention on the ceiling. There's a tea-colored stain directly over our heads. "Do you really like girls?" I swallow. "Like that I mean."

I mostly feel her nod rather than see it. "I've been questioning it for a while, but yeah, I think I do." She turns her head toward me. "What about you?"

"I don't know," I say. "How did you know?"

"How do you ever know you like anybody? It's different for everyone, but for me it was getting turned on at naked girls in movies. Then I realized I used to have this huge, fat crush on

Cherie." She laughs. "That lasted about a hot minute. She's far too straightlaced for me. And just plain straight."

I giggle. Actually fucking giggle. Dork.

Kate props herself on her elbow and looks at me. "Are you questioning your sexuality, Tabitha?" It sounds very after-school special to me, but Kate is dead serious.

"I uh… Well…"

"It's okay," she says. Her smile has turned into a smirk. "I have an idea. You don't have to answer. Just close your eyes."

My heart is about to beat right out of my chest, but I comply. I don't have a choice. My body is acting on its own. I no longer have free will. I'm only doing what I'm told. I can feel Kate coming closer, but I don't move, not a muscle, not an eyelash. I am frozen in time, waiting. For what I'm not sure.

Then her lips brush mine. Softly at first and then more firmly. My whole body is feverish as she cups my face in her hand. I don't know what else to do so I try to kiss back, but she's gone. When I open my eyes, she's still hovering over me; her hand covers her mouth. She's blushing, too.

Neither of us says anything, and Kate stands up and takes the tape out of the stereo. "I should probably get this back to Cherie." She looks at me lying on the floor. "I gotta pee. I'll meet you outside."

She climbs the stairs, and I lie there like a dumbstruck statue. I bring my hand to my lips, but they feel unchanged. And yet something is completely, irrevocably, unavoidably different. Something so life-changing, I don't know what to do with the information.

Plain and simple: I have a crush on Kate.

DECKED OUT NO. 2

HAVE IT YOUR WAY...OR THE OTHER WAY

BY KATE GOLDBERG

It seems like so many girls are bi these days—or pretending to be. I can't walk through the mall without bumping into at least six girls who want to hold hands and share chaste kisses with other girls. Where are all the girls who aren't afraid of being called a lesbian? Where are all the girls who want to drool over Claire Danes AND Jared Leto?

I am bisexual. Completely. Fully. I think boobs are hot. I used to dream about this girl in my 10th grade English class. Her name was Danielle and she had the most gorgeous body. And her smile. Her smile always made my day better. I tried to be her best friend but she already had one, a girl she had known since kindergarten. So I shelved my crush. Disregarded it as a need to be part of the cool group.

Later I dated this guy named Steve. He was edgy-skateboarder hot. He had long, shaggy hair and wore his pants low around his hips. We made out, and I let him feel me up because he gave me the same swoopy feeling in my tummy that Danielle had.

I kissed a girl the other day and it happened again—the swoop. Her name is Tabitha. She has the prettiest grayish-blue eyes, and I am smitten.

RULES FOR GIRLS IN THE '90S

1. Wear makeup.
2. Don't wear too much makeup.
3. Speak your mind.
4. Don't raise your voice.
5. Stand up straight.
6. Don't stick out your chest.
7. Dress modestly.
8. Be soft and feminine. Boys don't date tomboys.
9. Don't be too girly. Boys won't take you seriously.
10. BE WHATEVER YOU WANT TO BE THESE RULES ARE ARBITRARY!!!!!!!!!

OF MICE AND MENSES

BY CHERIE WONG

The masculinization of my period makes me want to bleed all over corporate America. I watch girls twirl around as their skirts magically become tampons that have white strings for tails like tiny cotton mice. Why do these advertisers think we all want to dance and leap while we are bleeding from our nether regions? Instead I dream about clear blue liquid floating away on the wings of a pad.

Who decided wings were something pads needed? Has anyone in product development every really worn these things? If you're lucky they stick to the side of your leg, but most of the time the little tabs just bunch up and pull out your pubic hairs. But no one talks about that because pubic hair is off limits. Sure, you can rip it out with your poorly designed maxi pad wings, but you can't f*cking talk about it, no.

And why the HELL is it called a sanitary napkin?

We have to dance and twirl and be happy about our periods while the blue liquid flows from a test tube because our uteri are commodified. Our bodies are for male consumption, not for bodily functions. Breasts are for ogling, not for feeding. Vaginas are for sex, not for giving birth. But wings are for birds and girls with small thighs. Tampons are for thin, pretty dancers who are quiet as mice. Periods are "that time of the month." I am bleeding and you want me to be happy?

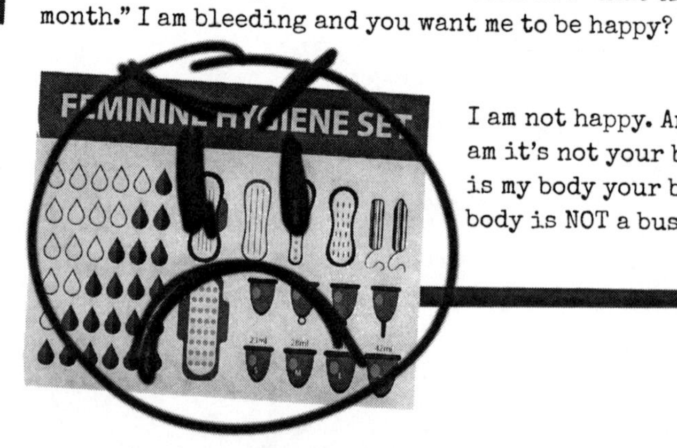

I am not happy. And even if I am it's not your business. Why is my body your business? My body is NOT a business.

CHAPTER 4

I DON'T TELL MIKE ABOUT Kate. I'm not sure why, but it feels like a betrayal. I mean, he knows we're friends, but if I tell him she kissed me, it won't be a secret anymore. And I don't know how Mike feels about me. I don't want to hurt his feelings. At least that's what I tell myself.

"You okay?" he asks. "You seem distracted."

I hate that he can see right through me. When did that happen? I don't remember us getting this close. What happened to hanging out behind the convenience store? I remember our almost-kiss and I shudder. How I feel about Kate is unrelated to how I feel about Mike, but right now the two seem inextricably linked.

"I didn't sleep very well," I lie. It's Sunday. I slept like a lazy housecat and didn't wake up until noon. He knows that. I do the same thing every Sunday.

Mike nods as if he's silently agreeing to believe my story even though he knows it's a fabrication.

"You've been hanging out with those chicks a lot lately." The way he says the word "chicks" sets my teeth on edge.

It's as though he's using it as a curse word, as if he's judging me.

"So?" I am barely containing my anger. Mike's judging me and he's judging my friends. Any affection I may have had dissipates in defense of my fellow Riot Grrrls.

"So nothing. It's just an observation. Jesus, you're in a mood today." He stamps out a cigarette and kicks the curb. The black scuff marks are still there from when I first wore my boots—an angry smudge that proves my existence, and yet I feel invisible. Mike doesn't see me for who I really am.

"Sorry." The word squeezes out through my sneer. I'm not sure why I'm apologizing. It's okay for me to be angry. Isn't it? I've always been a peacekeeper, though, and I simply want things to go back to normal between us. Before that almost-kiss that made me question the last year of my friendship with Mike. Before Kate kissed me and turned my world upside down. Why can't Mike just talk about music the way we used to? Or not talk at all? When did we start discussing our moods? I don't want to be here anymore. I ache for the solitude of my room and the pseudo-earthy smell of potato chips and the sticky tang of pop.

Mike breaks the silence first, but the tension stays. "Look, I'm gonna go. Why don't you call me when you're…" He trails off, the unsaid words hanging in the air between us.

"When I'm what?" I challenge.

"I don't know," Mike says. "Less angry. More Tabitha."

"This *is* me. Deal with it." I'm not sure where that came from but now that I've said it, I realize it's true and I walk away.

Does he know this is it for us? I won't call him. Things have changed. The Tabitha who needed Mike's friendship is gone.

The Tabitha seeking refuge from Heather's ire has grown up and moved on in the span of one girl-on-girl kiss. Her brief and misguided crush has gone up in smoke along with the tobacco in his cheap menthols. The new-and-improved Tabitha has better things to do. She has Kate.

KATE LINKS HER PINKY WITH mine as we enter the rec center. It's our first Riot Grrrl meeting as a "couple," and I'm nervous. What will Marty say? Will Cherie approve? Have they read Kate's zine?

Marty's on us before we're two steps inside the door.

"Look at the love birds!" Her hair is the color of grape Kool-Aid and smells like it too as she rushes up to give us a bear hug. My stomach lurches at the memory of my soaked gym clothes.

Kate must sense my tension because she squeezes my wrist. It's as comforting as she intended. Maybe more so.

"I can't believe you guys made out!" Marty looks like she just opened presents on Christmas morning. Okay, so she's definitely read Kate's zine.

"I can't believe you didn't tell us." Cherie's pout is insincere. She gives Kate a crushing hug, and our hands are tugged apart.

"It's not that big of a deal, guys." Kate's a pro at playing it cool, but my palms are sweaty. I wipe them on my jeans in case Kate wants to hold hands again.

"We didn't exactly make out," I mumble.

Ignoring me, Marty says, "I didn't know you played for the other team."

Kate jabs her with an elbow. "Rude."

"What? She walks in with you on her arm, and I can't call her a lesbian?"

"No, you can't," Kate says, her nose in the air.

"I don't mind," I mumble. It doesn't matter that Marty thinks I'm gay. Right now I want the attention off me and on something else. Anything else.

Kate turns to me and smiles. "Babe, only you can choose your labels. Don't let other people put you in a box, okay? We talked about this."

I take a deep breath. She's right. These girls won't judge me. Marty and Cherie are not Heather and Molly. Besides, I'm too busy soaking in the fact that Kate called me "babe" to care what anyone thinks. I clear my throat. "I guess I like girls," I say, barely loud enough for Marty to hear.

"Well, hallelujah!" Marty shouts. "Tabitha speaks."

I'm not sure why, but I've gotten a reputation as the shy one. Truth is, though, I rarely feel that way. Sometimes I just like to listen. I speak when I have something to say. Kate seems to have figured that out, but Marty is a bit more bullheaded. Kate's responding eye roll gives me courage.

"Oh, shut up, Marty. Just because I don't comment every time a bird farts doesn't mean I don't have a voice. Some of us know when to shut the hell up."

Kate squeezes me close and laughs. "See? My girl can stand up for herself."

Babe. My girl. I don't even know what Marty says in response.

As we're starting to stack the chairs, the doors to the rec center swing open, and three girls walk in. One of them is wearing a studded leather jacket. Her hair is pulled into tight rows of braids that fall halfway down her back. The tallest of the trio has legs that seem to go on for days and a loose afro that bounces when she walks. The third has a downturned mouth and bright, friendly eyes. When she catches me staring, she raises an eyebrow. Her buzzed hair makes her look butch and fierce. The rich and varied tones of their dark brown skin make me suddenly aware of how fair-skinned our group is.

"Is this Riot Grrrl?" Leather Jacket asks.

"Sure is, girlfriend," Marty says. She's trying too hard as usual.

The glare that Buzz Cut sends in her direction is armed with a thousand knives, and I'm glad she's turned her attention away from me so my heart rate can recover. Embarrassment keeps me silent as I catch her eye roll and stifle a laugh. She smiles in my direction, revealing bright white teeth. I catch myself staring, and my face burns as I turn to face Marty.

"We want to join," Leather Jacket says. She throws an arm around Buzz Cut. "I'm Venus and this is Jackie." She points to the tall girl with the Afro, "And Monique."

Kate steps in front of Marty and holds out her hand. "I'm sorry about Marty. Sometimes I swear she was raised by wolves." She laughs. "I'm Kate Goldberg. We just finished up but we're always happy to have new faces."

"We got lost or we would have been here earlier," Jackie says. I can't stop staring at her. She seems infinitely cool and it pulls me in like a moth to a flame.

"We didn't get lost," Venus says. "The address was wrong."

"Oh, we just moved," Marty says. "We used to meet at my house."

"Figures," Monique adds. "Two crazy white ladies have to be from the same family."

Marty gapes at her like a fish out of water. I've never seen Marty speechless. I bite my lip to keep from laughing.

"Your mom told us where you were," Venus clarifies.

Kate clears her throat. "Where do you girls go to school?"

"Central," Jackie says. "Me and Venus are seniors. Monique graduated last year."

"I think we had gym together." Cherie's voice is barely a squeak, and I had almost forgotten she was there.

Jackie raises an eyebrow. "Gym. Right." She rolls her eyes and huffs sharply. "Look, Vee, I think these Girl Scouts might be a little too vanilla for us."

"I take offense to that," Marty says. "We might be white, but we're definitely not vanilla." She thrusts her hands on her hips and gives Jackie her best punk glare. I can't believe I used to find Marty intimidating. It's hard to take her seriously when she's acting like a spoiled toddler.

"Oh yeah?" Venus looks like she's on the verge of laughter.

This time Cherie steps in front of Marty. "Why don't you come to our meeting next week? You can meet the other girls and make your minds up then."

"That's not a bad idea, Vee." Monique seems to be the voice of reason in their group, and for that I like her already. "And these girls seem cool. Anyone who will speak with Jack staring them down has to have *some* balls."

"Why does everyone always say that when they mean someone's tough?" Marty rants. "Shouldn't we say, 'She's got ovaries,' or something?"

Leave it to Marty to lose what little ground we gained in the last five minutes.

"Crazy girl's got a point," Jackie says. "Vaginas are way tougher than some saggy old balls."

Kate and I both turn to stare, open-mouthed, at Jackie.

"What?" she says, and the glare is back. "She's right."

Marty beams proudly. "I think we're going to get along just fine." Marty's too busy preening to see that the trio of girls are looking at her like she's nuts. She holds up her hand for a high five and says, "See you guys next Tuesday, then?"

A bored-looking Jackie says, "Sure, whatever." She ignores Marty's raised hand, but her body language has changed. She seems more relaxed. I take that as a good sign.

"Kate, I got to get home," I say. "My mom's going to flip if I'm late again."

"Sure thing, babe," she says and kisses my forehead.

I see Jackie's eyebrows rise, and my stomach flutters. I hope she's not offended. But I prepare myself to defend our relationship.

"Look, Jackie, you've found your fellow rug-munchers." Monique laughs.

I shoot glances from one to the other. From her appearance, I probably should have guessed Jackie was queer. But I had been too busy sneaking glances at Monique. I didn't realize until that moment that I'd been flirting. But the way she smirked when she teased Jackie says she's not on the same team. When I look back to Jackie, she's got her head down, and she's rummaging through her pockets.

"It's okay," I whisper. I'm not sure what's okay exactly, but it seems like the right thing to say.

Jackie's eyes meet mine and, beneath her cool exterior, I can see tears beginning to form. She blinks to hold them back the way I always do. I try to smile, but only one side of my mouth cooperates. I probably look like a moron.

"Thanks," she says, raising her head. She seems to regain some of her composure and all of her attitude. "Monique, stop being such a bitch, okay?"

Monique holds up her hands. "It was a joke. Jeez."

"We didn't find it very funny," I say. "And anyway, Kate and I are bi."

It's only the second time I've admitted it to myself and the first time I've said the word out loud. I brace myself for the laughter. It never comes. Jackie smiles at me, and her entire face lights up. She has a stunning smile. Monique rolls her eyes, and I think I might have to reconsider my initial impression of her. Kate simply threads her arm through mine and leads me to the car while I steal glances over my shoulder at Jackie.

When I close the door, I release a burst of air. I have to struggle to catch my breath.

"You okay?" Kate asks as she turns the key in the ignition.

"Kate," I say, my eyes glued to the dashboard, "I think I just came out to a complete stranger."

"Yeah, so?" She narrows her eyes at me. "Wait… was that the first time you said it? The word 'bi' I mean."

I nod. My face is hot but my hands are cold. My stomach flops around as though I drank a double espresso.

"How does it feel?"

I swallow. "I think I might throw up."

Kate's laughter is drowned out by the radio as I try not to burst into tears. Happy tears.

GIRLY DOESN'T MEAN WEAK!

Just because I wear lipstick and paint my nails doesn't mean I'm not a feminist and I wish people would figure that out. I shouldn't have to explain myself because these things make me feel good. I'm not doing it because the makeup ads say I have to. I'm not wearing designer jeans because some cracked-out supermodel told me to. I do this for me and it's none of your damn business.

I don't do it for boys and I won't stop doing it for girls. I do it for me. I like the way I look in eyeliner and lipstick. I like wearing sparkly nail polish. I don't have to cut my hair short and burn my bra, which by the way is lacy and pretty, just to prove something to the rest of you.

I'm starting a zine to prove that you can be a Material Grrrl and a feminist grrrl. I can be who I want to be. I'm going to include fashion tips and makeup recommendations and all-around "girly" stuff. Whatever stuff I'm into.

And if you don't like that, then you can, in the immortal words of Bikini Kill, "suck my left one." ~ Cherie Wong

P.S. You can subscribe to my zine, Material Grrrl, by writing to the address on the back. Just send $1 and two stamps.

★ And now, a special note from Marty, who promises not to swear...

I promise no such thing, but I'll try my best.

We'd love to see more of you at our Riot Grrrl meetings. We've moved to the Decker rec center on Collins so we have lots more room. I'm ready for a revolution and we need awesome girls like you. I promise it's not a clique or anything. We want as many girls in Decker to join as possible. Our youngest girls are in middle school and some of us are in college. There's no age limit. The only requirement to join is that you're a girl and you want to put a stop to all the girl hate in the world. We're girls supporting girls and WE WANT YOU.

Oh, by the way, Kate, Cherie and I are starting band rehearsals soon and we've narrowed our name down to two choices: Menstrual Weekend or The Claires. If anyone plays drums or guitar, we need a couple more chicks to round out our sound. Rock on! ~Marty

CHAPTER 5

"TABITHA, DID YOU WALK THE dog? I don't want him peeing on the carpet again." My mom's voice echoes up the stairs, and my heart stops.

"She's home early." My voice breaks on the last syllable. I freeze. My pants are unbuttoned and Kate is practically naked from the waist up. Her nipples stand erect through a lacy white bra. We've been making out for a good twenty minutes. "Shit." Mom doesn't know about me and Kate. She doesn't even know about me yet.

While I'm busy imitating a statue, Kate tugs her T-shirt back over her head and leaps off my bed. "I thought you said she wasn't getting home until seven."

Kate's voice pulls me out of my stupor. "She wasn't." I glance at my alarm clock. It's five forty-five. "She's never home this early."

"Never say never." Kate's breathless as she bends over to put on her shoes. Her hair is a matted mess in the back and her shirt is on backward.

"Kate, slow down. You look like…" I can't say the words.

"Like we've been making out?"

I nod, dumbfounded. I was making out with my girlfriend. Are we girlfriends? We haven't really had that talk. We've been too busy with our tongues in each other's mouths. And my tongue on her—

"Tabitha, will you—" My mom appears in my doorway and stares from me to Kate and back again. Her sentence hangs unfinished. "I didn't know you had company."

"Mom, this is Kate." *And she's a really good kisser.*

"Hi, Kate." Mom blinks and looks at me with a question in her eyes. Does she know? Can she see Kate's lipstick on my neck? Is it obvious that we've been making out half naked on my bed? I can't tell if my heart is beating double time or if it's skipping beats. Blood pounds in my ears, so it's definitely still working. Mom's eyes wander my room as if she's seeing it for the first time. Her gaze finally lands on Kate. "Do you go to school with Tabitha?"

"Um, no. I graduated last year."

My mom nods. She looks unsure of what to say next.

"I've really got to run," Kate says, her mouth drawn into a frown. Her lower lip forms a soft pout, and I notice her lipstick is completely gone. I rub the spot on my neck she had been kissing, hoping she didn't leave marks. "I'll call you later?"

I nod, but I really want to jump up and kiss her. I lock my fingers together to keep myself from moving. I shift nervously as I brace for my mom's questions.

When Kate is gone, my mother says, "She seems nice." Her awkward smile tells me she doesn't know what else to say. Margaret Denton is good at a lot of things: baking cookies, selling houses, running her own business and making a life for herself after a messy divorce. Not on that list: talking to her teenaged daughter. But at least she speaks to me. Dad hasn't called in two years.

"Did you want something?" I ask, rescuing her from herself.

"Oh, yes," she says as if she just remembered. "I'm going out tonight, so I left you some money on the counter for pizza."

"Out?"

"Yes."

"As in, a date?" I narrow my eyes at her. "So that's why you're home early."

Mom laughs and fidgets with a bracelet. "Well, sort of. I don't know. It might be a date."

I'm not sure about the etiquette here. Am I supposed to be a disgruntled teenager? Should I be supportive? Honestly, if she's happy I don't care. I just wish she'd told me this before Kate rushed out. We could have had the house to ourselves tonight.

"You going to be okay here by yourself?"

"Mom, I'm here by myself every day." I can't remember my mom ever being home before seven. I started staying home alone when I was in fifth grade, right after the divorce. I've had my own key to the house as long as I can remember. I learned to cook when I was eleven. I started doing my own laundry at thirteen. If I had my own car, I'd do the grocery shopping. I want to tell her about Kate and me. Instead I say, "Go. Have a good time."

She turns to go, but at the last minute she pauses in my doorway. "Um, if you want to invite Kate over, she's welcome any time."

"Okay."

"She's cute," Mom adds. "You're, uh… cute together?" She raises her voice on the last word as if she's testing out the phrase.

My heart beats double time. This time I can feel it, hot and persistent.

"Thanks." My voice comes out in a raspy whisper.

Mom nods. I'm not sure which of us feels more awkward. Finally, she says, "Okay. Money's on the counter. I should be home around eleven. I'll call if I'm going to be later than that." She steps back into my room and bends to scoop me up in a hug. "Love you, kid."

It takes me a second, but when my arms cooperate, I wrap them around her and squeeze hard. "Love you, too."

Despite her initial "acceptance," Mom doesn't mention Kate again. She's out a lot with this dentist named Dan, and I spend a lot of time with Kate. Our conversations happen in passing and through messages on our answering machine.

On Monday I come home to, "Hey, hon. I'm working late and then meeting Dan for dinner. There's leftovers in the fridge. I won't be late. Love you."

On Tuesday I call to say, "Hey, Mom, it's me. Kate and I are going to some lecture at the community college. I'll be home around eight-thirty."

Wednesday, I get home around nine to both my message saying Kate and I are grabbing a pizza and Mom's message saying she's out with Dan. She sticks her head in my room around eleven. I'm lying on my bed trying to finish my homework, but instead I'm doodling hearts in the margins of my notebook. I'm a sappy doofus. I don't think I care.

"Oh good. You're up," Mom says. "Sorry I'm so late. Did you have a good day?"

Her smile is sleepy but genuine. I haven't met Dan, but if he can make my mom smile like that, I guess he can't be all bad.

"It was good," I say. And for once it's not a lie. Kate and I ate out on what could almost be called a real date and then went to the park by my house and made out on the swings until it got too dark to see one another.

Even though we have the house to ourselves most evenings, Kate and I don't make out nearly enough—at least not in my opinion. Kate has other priorities, though.

Mom yawns. "Well, I think I'm going to go to bed. You need anything before I hit the hay?"

"Nope, I'm good."

She kisses the top of my head. "Good night. Don't stay up too late."

"I won't."

As soon as I hear her bedroom door close, I dial Kate's number.

She doesn't even say hello before asking, "Can you come to the protest tomorrow?"

I roll onto my back and throw my arm over my face. "I forgot to ask."

Kate sighs. "Tabitha, this is important. Don't you care about stopping animal testing?"

"Of course I do." And it's true. I don't think cosmetics companies should use animals to test toxic chemicals on cute little bunnies and mice. I've seen the pictures: tiny, helpless things with their eyes swollen shut; formerly fluffy creatures subjected to so many caustic substances that they're more raw meat than fur. It's awful. But at the same time, I highly doubt that a protest organized by six girls at Northeast Illinois Community College is going to change much. I have to bite my lip to keep from vocalizing that. "My mom got home late again and she's already in bed. I'll ask tomorrow morning."

"She probably won't notice anyway. It's not like she's been home any night this week."

Kate's right, but I can't help but get defensive at her tone. "She's been home."

"You know what I mean." I hear rustling in the background, and then Kate's stereo kicks on. "Look, I need to get some sleep. I'll pick you up after school, okay?"

I pause, waiting for her to say something else. Good night? I love you? I'm not sure what. The only noise coming over the line is the muted sound of The Slits' cover of "I Heard It Through the Grapevine."

Trying to say something more romantic than "bye" or "later," I whisper, "Sweet dreams."

"Huh?" Kate says. "I was changing my shirt."

"Never mind," I mumble. "Good night."

"Bye, Tab," she says.

There's a click and then silence. I can't decide if I feel empty or embarrassed. I grab a bag of Oreos I'd left on my desk and shove one in my mouth. Between bites of chocolate cookie and sugary frosting, I stop thinking and savor the fact that Kate had been expecting my call. I turn out the light and toss my books to the floor. I'll finish my homework in the morning. I keep the cookies nearby.

I HATE IT THAT KATE's right about my mom. She isn't home when Kate picks me up and she won't be home until late, so I dash off a quick note and hop in Kate's car. The crowd at the protest is bigger than I'd anticipated, and there are at least a dozen girls hoisting homemade signs sporting phrases like, "Fur on your back = Blood on your hands" and "Give voice to the voiceless!"

Kate pulls a sign from her trunk that reads, "Stop animal testing now!" in sparkly pink letters. She's decorated it with stickers of cartoon bunnies and mice.

"Cute."

"I thought it made a statement," she says. "Like how animal testing is not cute or something."

"Then why didn't you write that?"

"What?"

"Well, just say, 'Animal testing is not cute!' It gets straight to the point."

Kate sighs and shakes her head. "You so don't get it." She hands me the sign and slams her trunk before motioning for me to follow her to the group already forming on the steps of the campus's science building. A stout girl with light brown skin and dark, charcoal-lined eyes walks to the top step. Holding a megaphone to her lips, she shouts, "Stop animal testing now! Stop animal testing now!" She gestures for the crowd to join her, and Kate gives me a look that reeks of "told you so" as she parrots the chant. I hold up my hands in surrender and resign myself to marching in a circle while chanting that phrase repeatedly.

About an hour in, I have the beginnings of a sunburn, and my feet are covered in blisters. So I excuse myself to sit on the steps, which I hope will soon be in the shade of the science building. Kate urges me to keep chanting, though, so I sporadically repeat whatever the girl with the megaphone shouts. Every twenty minutes or so she changes the chant. Now we're on "Illinois is for animal lovers."

I kick off my shoes and let my hot, swollen feet recover from bearing my excessive weight. I wish I had remembered sunglasses. The sun is unusually hot for this time of year and shining directly in my face. I squint to try to make out the time on the clock mounted to the tower of the student union, and a shadow falls across my face.

"Hey, you."

It takes my eyes a moment to adjust but soon I can make out a familiar buzz cut and small, square-set shoulders. "Jackie Hardwick, right?"

She nods and sits beside me. "And you're Tabitha?"

I smile. "You remembered."

"Well, you made an impression."

My already pink cheeks flush even hotter, and I duck my head. "I was a little defensive that day. Sorry."

"Don't apologize," she says. "Marty was out of line."

I bite my lip. "She does that a lot."

"I figured." Jackie tilts her head back and closes her eyes. "Damn, that feels good."

"I wish I had remembered sunscreen. I'm going to be so burned tomorrow."

"That sucks. I hate getting sunburned."

Confused, I squint at Jackie. "You can get sunburned?"

She opens one eye and glances in my direction. "Yeeeees." She draws out the single syllable as if I've said the dumbest thing she's ever heard. I can see she's trying not to laugh.

I sputter as I try to find words that won't offend her or make me sound even more stupid. "But you're so— I mean, I thought— Um, is that—?"

"Yes, black people can get sunburned," she says in a monotone. "It just takes us a bit longer to burn, and we don't turn red, but we have *skin* and it can get darker." Both of her eyes are closed now, but there's tension in her jaw.

"I'm sorry," I say quietly. "Is that not okay to ask?"

She opens her eyes and studies me. Her expression shifts to something I can't read, and she sighs as her jaw relaxes.

"It's just a little tedious always having to explain myself."

I purse my lips. I'm afraid I'll say the wrong thing, but I have to say something. After the silence stretches between us long enough to feel awkward, I whisper, "I didn't know."

Jackie's only response is a close-lipped smile. It's not her warmest and most open expression, but considering that I can still taste the big, smelly foot I so gracefully stuck in my mouth, I'll take it.

I glance at Kate, who's still on the picket line, and see her watching me. When I wave, she tips her head at me and then shifts her gaze to Jackie. I allow my eyes to follow. But Jackie's eyes are still closed, with her head tilted back to take in the warmth of the sun that only moments ago had been the cause of tension. Calm and relaxed, she seems oblivious to Kate's attention. I study her. Her profile is stunning, actually. I can't believe I ever thought Monique was the pretty one. Jackie has the longest eyelashes I've ever seen, and even her delicate ears are cute. I can't help but smile and I hope that I haven't screwed up the possibility of friendship.

Kate's voice bellows above the rest, "Stop the testing! Stop the trials! Stop the testing! Stop the trials!"

I turn back to the protest to find Kate smiling at me and gesturing for me to join in. Reluctantly, I slip on my shoes.

"Where are you going?" Jackie's voice is husky and deep. It's seductive. I have to shake my head to clear it of inappropriate thoughts.

"Back to the grind," I say with a nervous laugh. I hope Jackie can't hear the tremor in my voice. Her body language is nonchalant, and her voice is sure all the time; I can't imagine what it must be like to be so confident. Quite frankly, I'm envious.

"Is this something you want to do?" she asks without opening her eyes.

I don't know if I do. I didn't really have a choice. Kate sort of dragged me along. "I want to be with Kate."

Jackie makes a small noise of acknowledgment but doesn't say anything. So I stand up and shuffle awkwardly before saying, "Well, I guess I'll see you Tuesday."

She opens her eyes and smiles. It's a full, genuine smile and it feels as warm as the sun on my back. "Bye, Tabitha," she says.

I can't explain it, but my name sounds important when she says it. My responding smile makes my sunburned cheeks ache.

Still grinning, I make my way back to Kate. When I'm close enough, she grabs my arm and links elbows with me. She smacks a loud kiss on my cheek and smiles through the chant. I look toward the steps, but Jackie is gone and I have to beat back my disappointment.

School still sucks, but man, is it a lot easier when you have friends and a *maybe* girlfriend to help you through. Heather remains on my periphery; she and Molly still lob insults in my direction every chance they get. But it's getting easier to shrug them off. When they taunt me with "Flabby Tabby" jokes, I write notes to Kate. And when that doesn't deflect the pain and embarrassment, I start my own zine to get out the bad thoughts that I can't share. Even though I know Kate and the other girls read it, it still gives me the illusion of privacy. There's a respect that goes along with the medium, and we all know the unspoken rules.

It's good to be able to trust girls again.

Guys, on the other hand? Well, for whatever reason they still have the ability to shift my entire world on its axis.

I'm coming out of first period, a little later than usual because Mrs. Sansone wanted to talk to me about taking some AP courses, and I run face-first into Brad Mason. He smells great as usual, and his dirty blond hair sweeps across his forehead in forced disarray, but he's looking at me strangely, as if he's never seen me before.

"Is Kate Goldberg your girlfriend?" he asks.

It's a simple question, but his tone makes the hairs on my arms stand at attention.

"I asked you a question, fatty," he says. His pale blue eyes narrow, and he uses his height advantage threateningly as he leans into my personal space.

Brad has always been a bit of a jerk, but he's never been outright cruel to me before. My hands begin to shake.

"Um, she's uh—"

"It's a simple yes or no. Are you a dyke or what?"

Somehow I manage to eke out three words. "I'm not gay."

"Could have fooled me." He pulls a crumpled sheet of notebook paper from his pocket. "I can't wait to see you," he says in a mocking tone. "I want to feel your lips on mine and your hands in my hair. I could kiss you for hours and never get bored."

I reach for the letter, and he snatches it away. "That's private!" I shout.

"What a waste." Brad clicks his tongue. "Kate is a fine piece of ass."

"What do you know about it?" My words are laced with venom, but my hands are still shaking and sweat drips down my back and pools at the base of my spine.

"Oh, I know plenty," he says. He leans over and I can smell his breath. It's the spicy-sweet smell of Big Red, and it makes my stomach turn. "Like how she has a birthmark right here." He touches my left breast just below the nipple. Where Kate has a tiny strawberry birthmark.

I forget to breathe.

"I think what you need," he says as he backs me toward the classroom door, "what you both need…" He brings his hands up to frame my face, trapping me against it. "Is a man."

I close my eyes and pray. For what I don't know. That I get out of this with my dignity intact? That he leaves me alone? That he hasn't seen Kate naked?

Before I can figure it out, he surges forward and crushes his lips against mine. It hurts. There's no tenderness—just pain and fear and an overwhelming urge to run away. I try to push him off, but he's stronger than me. In the back of my mind, I know he won't do anything. We're at school, and he's not stupid. But my body reacts faster than my brain. I panic. White-hot stars pepper my vision, and I can feel myself being dragged under. I hope it happens soon. Then I won't be here with Brad's cinnamon breath engulfing my entire face.

As I'm slipping out of consciousness, I realize he's gone. When I open my eyes, Mrs. Sansone is standing next to us; her fist is full of Brad Mason's shirt.

"What the hell is going on here?" she demands.

"We were just having a little fun, right, Tabitha?"

I can't speak. I think my knees might give out, and I'm struggling to breathe.

"It didn't look like Miss Denton was having fun," she says. "I think you'd better come with me to the dean's office." She smiles at me. In her gaze, pity prickles sharply where there once was pride. I look away. "Why don't you go to the nurse's office, dear? Have your parents come pick you up."

I nod. I can't remember any words. I look up to see Brad glaring at me over his shoulder as Mrs. Sansone drags him off. When they're out of sight, I sag against the door. My whole body begins to shake, and I swallow to force down the bile in my throat.

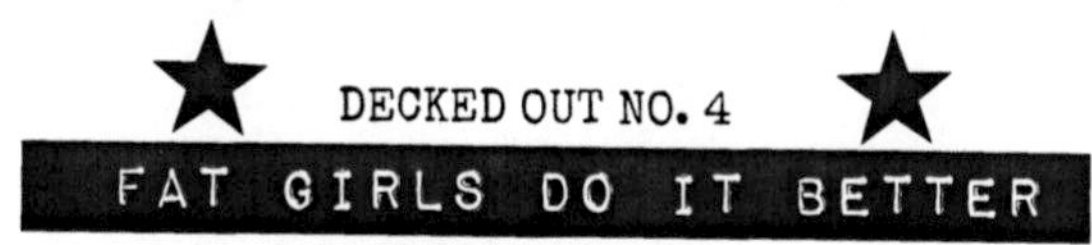

BY TABITHA DENTON

This is my big fat body and it's mine. I inhabit it fully and freely. You can't take that from me. I eat and I live. I live and I eat. But only one of these things defines me. I also love. I have love to give.

Sometimes I feel invisible, even though I know I physically take up more space than most girls. Sometimes that's fine. I want to be invisible. I don't want you to see my fat rolls and stretchmarks and cellulite. Other days I want to scream "HERE I AM! LOOK AT ME!" as I squeeze my stomach and make you feel the thickness of my body. This is what it's like to be fat, what it's like to be me. I demand that you notice me.

The only problem is when I get noticed. When I'm seen for who and what I am. When I'm taunted for my size, for whom I love. For how I love.

"You need a man..." Those words burn through me and eat away at my insides until I can hardly breathe. Why does everyone think they have a right to your body? Especially guys. I am not a product for consumption. I am a human being. I have feelings and rights the same as you.

Every fat joke eats away at my pride; every sneer at me and my girlfriend makes me angrier. My anger guides me; it makes me stronger. I will eat you and your skinny friends. I will make you take me seriously. And I will do it all while being fat.

Because. I. Can.

It's Time to Slim Down the Easy Way
Debbie lost 20 pounds on our easy, no-fuss program.

★ DEBBIE IS A SELLOUT!

If you want more fat girl love, write to the address on the back to subscribe to Tabitha's zine, Chubby Bunny. It's just $1 and two stamps for all the feminist propaganda you can stand.

CHAPTER 6

"HE DID *WHAT?*" KATE'S HEART-SHAPED face is contorted in pure rage.

"It's nothing," I say. "I'm fine." I'm not sure if I'm actually fine. I'm only saying that so Kate doesn't drive across town and kick Brad in the balls. From the look on her face, it's still a possibility. And not that I'd blame her, but I'd rather forget the whole stupid thing. Now that the immediate threat is gone, it seems silly that I've been scared.

"It's not fine," she says. "How dare he!"

"I'm really okay," I say again. "He didn't hurt me." Except he did. There might not be any physical scars, but in the few days since it happened, the smell of cinnamon has begun to make me queasy, and the squeak of sneakers in the hallway has been making me jump.

Kate begins to pace back and forth as she mutters something to herself. I have to say something to stop her from doing anything rash.

"Kate?" I try to step in front of her, but she dodges me and continues her route across my bedroom floor.

She scowls at the floor. "It's none of his business who I date! We broke up a year ago for crying out loud."

"Wait. What?" Something is wrong. Why does she care what Brad thinks?

"He always was jealous," Kate says, almost to herself. "But this is crossing the line."

"Are you even listening to me?" I practically yell to get her attention.

"Yeah," she says, finally looking at me again. "Brad was being a jealous dumbass and confronted you."

"Kate, he kissed me." I take a couple steps in her direction and put my hands on her shoulders. "He forced himself on me and he threatened me… he threatened *us*."

"That's just him," she says, waving it off. "He's… possessive."

"So that makes it okay?"

"No, but…" When she catches my pained expression, she softens her voice and kisses me. "Tabitha, he's harmless."

"It didn't *feel* harmless," I say as I fight back tears. How can she see this as anything but a violation of my person? Of our relationship? Of everything we stand for?

"He's just trying to get to me through you," she insists. "I'll talk to him. He'll leave you alone. Promise." She holds out a pinky for me to link with hers but I stare at it in disbelief.

"You're going to *talk* to him?" I can't imagine on what planet she'd think it's okay to talk to a guy who assaulted her girlfriend, but then again, we've never had "the talk." Maybe I'm not her girlfriend after all.

"Oh my God, Tabitha, you are so immature sometimes." She throws her hands up. "He's an ex. It's no big deal."

"I don't care that he's your ex," I say, although I'm not quite sure I believe it myself. "I don't want him to hurt you."

"For crying out loud, Tabitha. He's not going to hurt me. I swear, you're such a child."

I step back. How can she say that to me when this guy forced his tongue in my mouth? When she's sat in the same Riot Grrrl meetings I have and heard the same stories? How can she not see this as a complete and total violation? "I'm not a fucking child," I say through gritted teeth. "He assaulted me!"

"Don't you think you're overreacting a bit?" Kate rolls her eyes, and that breaks something loose inside me. I cross my bedroom in three strides and yank the door open.

"I think you should go."

Kate stares at me with her mouth open. When I don't move, she picks up her shoes and her bag from my floor.

"Fine. You know what? I'm going, but don't think you can call me in five minutes and beg me to come back. You owe me an apology!" I think I see her eyes well up as she walks past me, but she doesn't even pause.

My legs turn to jelly when I hear the front door slam.

THE FOLLOWING TUESDAY, I'M THE only one in the rec center when Jackie and Venus walk in. Sitting in the lone chair I've bothered to take out, I'm debating whether I should stay. It's been three days since my fight with Kate, and she still hasn't called me. Pride keeps me from dialing her number. And today I can't decide if I want to see her. She may not even show up. It would be a betrayal to share what happened between us with the group.

"Well, this is one pitiful party," Jackie says. Her smirk seems playful, as if she's inviting me to reply, but I can't. Even the *thought* of speaking makes the tears threaten to flow. How do I have any tears left? I went through so much Kleenex over the weekend, Mom thought I was sick. Why am I so broken up over a two-week relationship?

I stand and clear my throat. "I didn't realize how late it was. I should set up."

"We'll help," Venus says. "How many chairs do we need?"

"Um, about fifteen, I guess."

Jackie is setting the last chair in the circle when Kate breezes through the door with Cherie in tow. My heartbeat pounds in my ears as Cherie waves and Kate looks past me to Jackie and Venus. When Kate turns, I can see she has shaved the side of her head, and her rusty brown hair now hangs in loose waves down one side. Her smile, aimed at anyone but me and framed by red lipstick, makes my chest ache. Tears sting my eyes, and I bite my lip to keep it from quivering.

A hand grips my elbow, and Jackie whispers in my ear, "Come with me."

I let her lead me out and around the side of the building. She nudges me toward a picnic table dotted with unidentifiable stains and streaked with bird droppings. The filth is fitting somehow as I sit across from Jackie and let my tears fall. I am about as useful as a mound of trash.

She lets me cry it out. When I sniffle and wipe my face she says, "Breakups suck."

I laugh bitterly. "I don't even know if we're broken up."

"Well, she's definitely ignoring you, and that also sucks."

"It really sucks." My eyes are locked on a particularly large bird dropping.

Jackie tilts her head down to meet my gaze. "Do you want to talk about it?"

Her eyes are laced with flecks of gold that sparkle when the light catches them. I hadn't noticed that. The trees flutter with the lightest spring breeze, and the sunlight dances over us. I take a deep breath.

"We had a fight," I begin.

Jackie listens while I tell her about the incident with Brad and my subsequent fight with Kate; she doesn't say a word until I stop talking. I wait for her to say something, expecting her to tell me I overreacted, or maybe that Brad is a bastard or that Kate isn't worth it.

Instead, she holds my hand.

BEING IGNORED BY KATE GETS easier. Jackie distracts me whenever she's around, and Marty has consumed most of Kate's time with the band, which has its first gig in a week. We've all sort of become roadies because the band usually practices after the Riot Grrrl meetings. They're pretty good when Marty's not yelling at Venus for playing too loudly, which is what is happening now.

"I can't hear myself think," Marty shouts over the driving beat of the band's only original song. It's a reworking of "Never Again," the song we sang at my first Riot Grrrl meeting. Marty has renamed it "Fuck the Man."

"You're not supposed to," Venus yells back. "It's punk. It's supposed to be loud and in your face."

She's a great drummer, but she enjoys annoying Marty a little too much.

"Let's just get through the song," Kate says into the mic. When she plays, her hair falls in front of her face and it reminds me of making out in my bed. She'd lie on top of me and her hair would fall exactly like that, framing our faces and hiding us from the world.

"Pining will get you nowhere." Jackie sidles up to me and nudges my hip.

"I'm not pining," I say. At Jackie's pointed look, I add, "Not exactly. I'm just remembering… fondly."

"That's just another name for the same damn thing, and it ain't healthy."

"I keep thinking she'll come around and we can at least be friends again." I kick the ground hard. The dead animal smell finally wore off my boots and I've started wearing them again, so I'm savoring the weight and heft of the steel toes. "I miss her."

"Doesn't look like Miss Fussypants returns that sentiment." Jackie nods at the stage. Kate is facing Cherie and banging her head in time with the music. She sticks her tongue out, and Cherie giggles. They seem to be having the time of their lives. Kate plays the same note on her bass, over and over, driving beat after driving beat. Cherie's vocals are haunting and rage-filled as she sings, "We are women who won't be silenced." Marty plays as if she's racing to the finish on the back of a minor chord. And behind the drum kit, Venus's braids swing in a tornado of hair as her sticks thump out a frantic beat.

When it's over, Marty steps to the mic and says, "Thank you. We're Menstrual Weekend."

Venus slams her sticks on the snare, and the sound echoes through the nearly empty room. "I told you I am not getting up on the stage in front of a bunch of people who are thinking of nasty old used tampons!"

"It's a *fierce* name. No one is going to be thinking of tampons, right, Tabitha?" Marty turns toward me.

I shrug. "Well…"

"She's not even in the band," Venus says. "Cherie, you're with me on this, right?"

"I liked The Claires," Cherie says timidly.

"Like we're some place to get your ears pierced at the mall? No way." Marty's nostrils flare and she glares at Cherie. Ducking behind her microphone, Cherie pretends to be enthralled by a spot on the floor. Marty sighs. "Kate, what about you?"

"I never really liked either of them. I thought you were joking about Menstrual Weekend."

"We need a fucking name," Marty says. "The show's next week."

"What about 'Shut Up'?" Jackie smirks in my direction.

I laugh, but none of the girls onstage join me.

"Actually, Jacks, that's a really good idea," Venus says.

"I have to say, it's not half bad," Marty adds.

Cherie smiles and nods excitedly, and Kate steps up to her mic. "Hello, we're called Shut Up." She plays a three-note lick and adds, "Let's rock!"

"It works," I say over the whoops and yells of the band. "You actually got them to stop arguing and—"

Jackie cuts me off: "Shut up."

We're both laughing so hard we barely notice that they've started their second song.

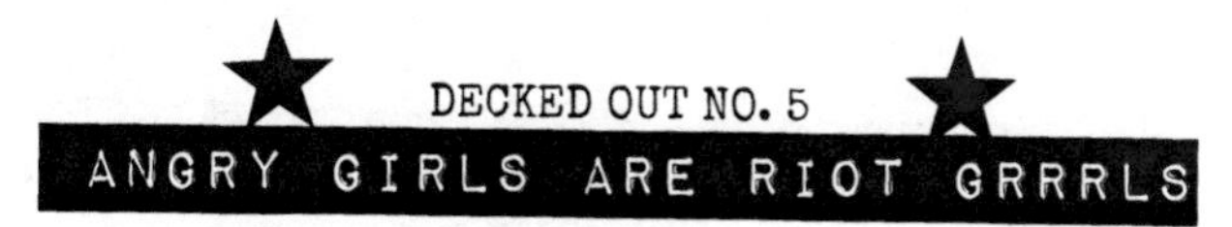

DECKED OUT NO. 5

ANGRY GIRLS ARE RIOT GRRRLS

BY MARTY DEVANE

I keep writing all this shit for everyone else's zines so I figured it was time to start my own. I was going to name it after our band, Shut Up, but I decided if that goes tits up, I'd better have a backup plan. So welcome to the first-ever glimpse into Rage Mart. I'm your notorious host Marty and I play guitar. Shut Up is going to be playing the Decker Spring Fest next week along with Lipstick Revolver and a few other really great local punk bands. Admission is only $5 for the entire weekend so you better get your ass over to the fairgrounds and be ready to rock your faces off.

We're going to have tapes of our first song, "Fuck the Man," available for purchase. We've included a few covers so the price of $5 is a little more fair. But don't tell the record labels or they'll sue us for our shitty secondhand amps and Cherie's blue nail polish. Honestly that's all we got right now. I'm hoping we can make some scratch with this band thing so I can afford to move out of my mom's house. She's such a bitch sometimes. She won't even let me practice in the house. Can you believe it? You know how some famous musicians pay off their parents' mortgages when they make it? Not me. She can continue to pay for that shit hole on her own while dad sleeps away his life.

Anyway... Binn County Fairgrounds, this Saturday at 7pm. BE THERE!!!

Oh and some of you bitches should be reading my zine, Rage Mart. You know the drill. Two stamps. One dollar. Angry feminist prose.

FUCK THE MAN

(LYRICS) BY MARTY DEVANE AND CHERIE WONG

It started on a cold night in September;
He looked at me so strange.
I tried to tell him it was over;
He took my hope and made it rain.

Chorus:
Fuck the man;
fuck my uncle;
fuck it all my friend.
We are women who won't be silenced,
never again the end.

After, I ate a hundred ripe raspberries;
Then I stole a blue canoe;
And I took my shoes off in the water;
With nothing else to do.

Chorus

When it was all over,
I tried to tell someone.
I had no reason to be a liar,
And yet you called me one.

Chorus

Never again, the end. (Repeat 5 times)

♀♡♀ CHAPTER 7 ★★★

I PLAN TO GO TO Spring Fest with Jackie and Monique because Jackie's the only other Riot Grrrl I know with a car. But at the last minute, Monique backs out. Her aunt died, and she has to go to the funeral in Chicago, so it's just me and Jackie. It's fine with me because I like hanging out when it's only the two of us. Jackie is funny; her dry sense of humor keeps me from being intimidated by how cool she is. Mostly.

"I hate the way people drive around here," she yells. "Use your stupid turn signal!"

"Turn signal? Is that the stick attached to the steering wheel? Or the big honky thing in the middle?"

Jackie fights the smile playing at her lips. "Ha, ha," she deadpans. "You're soooo funny."

"I'm hilarious."

"Then why am I not laughing?"

"Because you're a stick in the mud," I say matter-of-factly. Then turning serious, "Why don't you smile more?"

Jackie's driving so she can't turn her head, but her eyes shoot in my direction.

My heart flutters as my own words reach my brain. "Shit. I didn't mean it like that," I say. "You don't *have* to smile. I just meant that I, um…" I turn to look out the window to hide my blush and to stop myself from blurting out that I think she has the most beautiful smile I've ever seen. "You seem sad sometimes."

Jackie clears her throat. "I'm not sad." After a few moments, she adds, "I guess I don't feel like I have a lot to smile about."

Her eyes dart in my direction again as if she's gauging my reaction.

"What do you mean?" I ask.

She sighs. It's a little like exasperation. Maybe I've asked the wrong question again. But before I can apologize, she answers.

"In case you haven't noticed, I'm black. I'm a lesbian, *and* I live in the whitest of the white suburbs. It's not exactly where I'd like to be."

"Where would you like to be?"

"Chicago. New York. Hell, I'd settle for Cincinnati. Anywhere but here."

"I can understand that."

"Can you?" Her words come out clipped. Her mouth tenses. It's a subtle difference, but even after a few short weeks, I've noticed that's the first sign that she's frustrated.

Again, my mouth works before my brain, and I ask, "Are you mad at me?" I want to smack my head on the dashboard as soon as it comes out. And my voice is shaking. Great.

We're stopped at a light so she turns to look at me. "No, I'm not mad. I just don't think you get it."

I open my mouth to object, but she holds up a finger. It brushes my lips.

"Can we talk about something else?" she whispers. "I don't want to get in a fight."

I want to ask her what she means, but I stop myself. If she wants to change the subject, I will. Obviously something is bothering her, and if she's not ready to talk about it, I won't force her. I hate when someone does that to me. And maybe the best way to prove to her that I get it is to respect her wishes. I bite my lip.

"We could listen to some music," I suggest as I dig in my bag for the tape I brought.

Jackie ejects whatever is in the player and takes the tape. Without even asking what it is, she pushes it in.

As the frantic beat of a Joan Jett song fills the car, Jackie drums on the steering wheel. The tension is gone from her jaw. Knowing that she let me in a little bit makes my stomach do a flip, and, in a moment of bravery, I reach across the center console and put my hand over hers.

Because they're the first act, Shut Up only plays to about twenty or thirty people, which is about a dozen more than we expected. Jackie and I make our way to the stage, stationing ourselves immediately in front of the band where they'll be sure to see us. I wave to a couple girls I recognize from the rec center and motion for them to come to the front with us. This is a Riot Grrrl show as much as it's a Shut Up show. The girls should be front and center.

When the band finally takes the stage, there are eleven of us in the front row, thrashing and singing along to "Fuck the Man." Before long, some girls we don't know join us as Shut Up launches into their first cover: Bikini Kill's "Rebel Girl."

Something about that song in this moment takes me out of myself, and it's clear that Riot Grrrl is so much bigger than our little group in tiny Decker, Illinois. I look at the girls around me—dancing, singing, laughing. The connection is like an electrical current running through us. We are part of something, and it's pretty darn special.

SHUT UP'S SET IS ONLY fifteen minutes long. Most of the songs are covers, but Marty declares it a success.

"Let's go for pizza to celebrate!" She throws an arm around Venus, who looks ready to throttle her. "Or bowling. The bowling alley in Stuckey has that black light thing Saturday nights. We could all wear white and glow like we have radiation poisoning."

"I don't think that's how that works," Cherie says. "And anyway, I've got to get home. Mom wants me to babysit the twins so she and Dad can go look at new cars."

"The glamorous lives of freshly minted rock stars," Kate says with a self-deprecating laugh. "Bowling and babysitting."

"I'd be down for pizza," Venus says, "but bowling is out of the question. No way I'm wearing shoes that someone else's stank feet have been in."

"Fine. Whatever." Marty's arm drops from Venus's shoulder, and she places both hands on her hips. "We'll do boring old pizza then. Kate, you coming?"

"Let me drop Cherie at home and I'll meet you there."

"Sure," Marty says, her smile unflagging as she turns to me and Jackie. "You guys can come too. I know you're not *officially* in the band, but since you kind of named us..." She trails off.

"What a warm and friendly invitation," Jackie says in a monotone.

"What is everyone's damage today?" Marty says in exasperation. "We just rocked this thing and you guys are acting like we played checkers all afternoon."

"There *was* a lot of black-and-red flannel out there," I admit. "Maybe it was a game of checkers in disguise."

Jackie snickers. "Not helping," she mutters.

I bite my lip to keep from giggling.

"Let's go," Marty says. "We'll meet you at Vincenzo's in thirty, okay?"

Kate is already halfway to her car with Venus and Cherie in tow, so only Jackie and I are left to agree.

When Marty follows, Jackie turns to me and cocks her head to the side as though she's studying me. "You okay?"

Unsure of what she means, I ask, "Why wouldn't I be?"

"I don't know. Seeing Kate again. You've kind of been avoiding her. I thought maybe it was still a sore spot."

"I don't think I've been avoiding her. Have I?" I'm not playing dumb. I hadn't realized. I somehow had stopped thinking about Kate. Huh.

Jackie shrugs. "Maybe you've moved on?"

Her questioning tone makes me self-conscious. Maybe I'm suppressing latent feelings or something. "Was it too quick?"

Jackie bites her lip. "No, it's good I think. Just steer clear of rebounds."

"I don't think I have anything to worry about there." I hold my hands up in surrender. "I'm done dating for a while."

Jackie raises an eyebrow. "Never say never."

"Well, not never. Just not now… and definitely not Kate."

"Definitely." Jackie's smile lights up her face.

THE BAND, LOUD AND RAUCOUS, is still riding their performance high when we arrive, and a few other Riot Grrrls—Jenny and Becky are tucked into the end of the booth next to Venus—have joined them. I let Jackie lead me to the table and squeeze into the booth next to her. It's a little cramped, but instead of being uncomfortable, I feel safe. For the first time in my life it's as though I'm right where I belong—with these girls, who not only share my interests but who also *want* to hang out with me.

"So I was thinking," Marty says. "Maybe we get more girls contributing to *Decked Out*. It's not like we're going to have all this time on our hands if Shut Up keeps getting gigs."

"That's not a bad idea," Kate says. "It would give us more time to write music if we're not so focused on the zine."

"I'd love to write something on the pressures of being an honor student *and* female," Jenny says as she tosses a piece of crust onto her plate. "I get sick of having to be perfect all the time. God forbid I get a B or don't look cute while doing it."

It's unreal. I thought I was the only one. I had no idea Jenny felt pressure like that, too. I smile at her and take a sip of my pop.

"It *would* be nice to play more originals," Venus adds. "I know I'm sick of doing covers. But I'd still like to write stuff for the zine."

"I don't see why we can't do both," Kate says.

"What's wrong with covers?" Marty asks with raised eyebrows.

Venus sighs. "I'm not saying we *shouldn't* play covers, I'm just saying we should write more original songs."

"Are you going to write these songs, Vee? Because if it's all going to fall on me and Cherie to do the writing, we're going to have to play some fucking covers." Marty is riled up. She's talking with her hands and speaking at full volume. She and Venus never seem to agree, and, for whatever reason, Marty won't let an argument go.

"Does anyone mind if we change the subject?" Kate says, raising her voice to be heard over Marty. "This is getting tedious."

"Sure," Marty says with a sneer. "Why don't we talk about what happened with you and Tabitha."

I half-choke on a bite of pizza. Jackie places her hand on my thigh and offers me a sip of her Coke. I chance a sideways glance at Kate, but she's focused on glaring at Marty.

"Wow, you really know how to turn a party into a funeral," Jackie says. "Great job." She moves her hand to my back and rubs it until I stop coughing.

"Why don't you mind your own business for once?" Kate says under her breath.

"That better be directed at Marty," Jackie warns.

"Or what?"

Jackie shakes her head, "Never mind. It's not my problem."

Kate sits up and tilts her head. "No, I want to know. What did I ever do to you?"

Jackie stands up, but I touch her wrist in an attempt to comfort her. "I'm not wasting my breath. It's not like you'd listen to me anyway."

Kate scoffs into her pop. "Whatever."

Jackie's jaw tenses for a split second, but then she shakes her head as if she's shaking off Kate altogether. Under my grip, Jackie's hand balls into a tight fist, and her pink palms turn almost as pale as mine. But she's not preparing to fight. She's nervous; her hands are shaking. I rub my thumb across the inside of her wrist and hope she knows what I'm saying with the gesture.

But Jackie remains standing, using all of her five feet, two inches to show Kate she's not giving up, but she is walking away. "Tabitha, let's just go," she says.

Her eyes meet mine, and I mouth, "Okay."

Her body remains tense, but the left side of her mouth twitches up just enough that I can tell she's glad I'm ready to go. When I stand up, I slip my hand into hers, the way she did to me that day on the picnic bench. It takes a moment, but she relaxes and twines her fingers between mine. She turns back to the group.

"Tabitha and I are leaving," she says. "See you at home, Vee."

Without sparing a look for Kate, I follow Jackie out of the restaurant. She doesn't say a word until she pulls into my driveway.

"Thanks," she says without looking at me.

"For what?" I should be thanking *her*.

"For being there for me."

I shrug. "I could tell you were upset, and Kate's not worth it. Anyway, it's the least I could do after you stood up for me."

"Just because you're quiet doesn't mean they should walk all over you."

"Marty's just got a big mouth. I'm used to it."

She finally turns her head to face me. "You shouldn't have to get used to it."

"They're my friends."

"Doesn't mean they get to treat you like shit."

"They don't treat me like shit." I turn and stare out the window. Our lawn needs mowing. "Not usually."

"I'm just saying it's okay to stand up for yourself. You don't have to take it."

The thick grass on our lawn blurs as tears burn my eyes. I blink to keep them at bay. "I'm working on it," I say softly.

Jackie reaches across the console and squeezes my hand. I turn to her and half smile. "Thanks."

She smiles back. "Ditto."

I open the car door and walk up to my house. When I look over my shoulder, Jackie waves and waits until I'm safely inside. My stomach flutters, and I try not to think about it.

After that, my friendship with Jackie blooms quickly. Where Kate once held my attention, now Jackie occupies my thoughts. I wonder if I'm developing a crush on her like I did with Kate, but Jackie never tries to kiss me the way Kate did. So maybe she's not interested, and I meant what I said. I'm not looking for another girlfriend or boyfriend right away. Besides, Jackie can get anyone she wants. Hell, she's already been asked out by three different Riot Grrrls, all of whom she declined while I stood by in shock. I wish I had the kind of magnetic pull that Jackie has. But I'm just me.

At school I'm more invisible than ever, which ordinarily would be fine. It's easier to sneak by if you blend in. Despite the monotony of school, I'm bracing myself for impact, as if something big is coming. Heather and the rest of the Chick

Clique mostly leave me alone, but I still sense their eyes on me and hear their snickers behind my back. It's unsettling. With Kate in my rearview, and Mike out of the picture, I'm untethered, like a stray balloon floating through the sky. Jackie seems willing to pick up the slack.

She rings my doorbell one Saturday afternoon, toting a ratty blue backpack over one shoulder. Despite the warm spring weather, Jackie wears a leather jacket that swallows her narrow shoulders and weighs down her slight frame. She looks tough in that jacket, unless she smiles. But when she does, her cheek-splitting grin is childlike and contagious. It lights up her entire face and erases even the slightest hint of a frown. It's as though she's two entirely different people, and I want to get to know them both.

"Hey," she says, beaming at me. I can't help but smile back. "I thought maybe we could hang out."

I look down at my flannel pajama pants and battered *Ren & Stimpy* T-shirt. "I need to get dressed."

"Is that a yes?" She seems uncertain, almost as if she's afraid of rejection. How is that possible?

"Yes," I say. It comes out a little breathy, almost like a laugh. "Come in."

I hold the door open and Jackie squeezes past me into our living room, tossing her backpack to the floor and herself in a chair.

"I, uh. I'll just be a minute." I motion toward the stairs.

"I'll be here," Jackie says. Seeming sure of herself again, she pulls a paperback from her jacket pocket and molds herself to the softness of my dad's recliner. Mom and I never use it. It sits there mocking us with the memory of a man who no longer wanted it or us. I'm not sure why my mom hasn't gotten rid of it, but knowing her, she hasn't noticed. The chair has always been here and so it stays. With Jackie sitting in it, the chair seems more out of place in our home than ever. Her style seems at odds with the Middle America-ness of a faded blue recliner. She should be waiting for the subway in a sprawling city, not sitting in a living room in the middle of suburbia. She's too cool for Dad's chair… and for me.

"I'm fine if you want to wear flannel, but maybe pick a shirt that doesn't have holes in it," Jackie says without looking up from her book. She smirks and turns a page.

Was that flirting? With me? My stomach flips at the thought. As I back out of the room, I tug at the edge of my shirt, where the largest hole reveals a pale swath of my huge belly. I'm suddenly keenly aware of my appearance and wish, not for the first time, that I could disappear into the carpet.

In the time it takes me to stumble upstairs and find something less embarrassing to wear, Jackie has finished whatever she'd been reading and is now browsing one of the bookshelves flanking the fireplace.

"You were a cute kid," she says at the sound of my footsteps.

"Thanks," I mutter, hoping she missed the fifth-grade snapshot of me with a hideously bad perm. "So where are we going?"

Jackie places the photo she's examining back on the shelf. "I didn't have anything specific in mind. We could go for a walk?"

In a response that would shock even Pavlov, Sparky trots into the room. His ears perk up, and he pants, looking from me to Jackie.

"He heard the word 'walk,'" I explain.

At the second mention, Sparky barks and jumps, making repeated half-runs toward his leash.

Jackie bends to scratch behind Sparky's ears as she coos, "Good boy." Sparky revels in the attention and slobbers all over her hand as she laughs. "We can take him with us," she says to me. "I like dogs."

At least I'll have something to distract me from the bit of midriff showing between Jackie's jeans and her T-shirt. The jacket had covered it before, but now I can see her tiny nub of a bellybutton peeking out. I've never seen an outie before, maybe that's why I can't stop staring. Her skin is a smooth, bronze mystery that I want to solve. A familiar flutter in my belly forces me to look away and focus on finding Sparky's leash.

When I find it on the kitchen counter, Sparky runs at the door, yapping and panting louder than before.

"Dumb dog," I say, struggling to attach the leash to his collar.

"I think he's sweet," Jackie says.

"Just wait until he starts chasing squirrels. He can't decide if he wants to catch them or if they're trying to kill him."

"We had a dog that used to suck on his tail," Jackie says. "A certified genius, that one."

"What happened to him?"

"Hit by a car," Jackie says.

"Oh, how awful."

"Not really. I mean, we were upset and all, but he was almost sixteen… and barely able to walk when it happened." She shrugs, but I can see the memory is painful. "It saved us the cost of having him put down."

"Were you...? I mean..." I catch myself, but I can tell from Jackie's expression she knew what I was going to ask.

"No, we weren't poor," Jackie says. "Just because I'm black doesn't mean I'm from the projects. I grew up in a nice part of Chicago. My dad is an accountant. My mom teaches Sunday school. And, yes, they're still married."

"I didn't mean—"

"I know you didn't, but you did assume, didn't you?"

I nod shamefully. I'd unfairly assumed Jackie came from a poor, inner-city neighborhood. Everything about her seems so urban and worldly. And as much as it pains me to admit, I've always equated black kids with cities and white kids with the suburbs. There are a few non-white kids at my high school, but not many. Jackie is the first girl I've been friends with who didn't look like me and everyone else in Decker. "I'm sorry," I say finally.

Jackie shrugs. "I just don't like being stereotyped."

"No one does." I think of all the jabs thrown at me for my weight and how everyone assumes I eat nonstop and that I'm lazy or that I'm going to die young. None of it's fair... or true. I'm still a person—a living, breathing person—and not a caricature.

"No, I suppose not."

We walk in silence, taking a left at the end of the cul-de-sac and heading toward the park, where I can let Sparky off his leash inside the fenced area. As soon as he realizes where we're headed, he tugs sharply on the lead, jerking me forward and off balance. I catch myself with a flapping sound of rubber soles against the sidewalk. I stumble against Jackie, and she catches me with a strong grip.

"Easy there," she says.

My skin burns at her contact. It's not an unpleasant sensation, but it catches me off guard and Sparky's leash slips from my hand.

"Sparky! Get back here!" I shout. But he's gone like a dart, taking off through someone's yard with his bright red leash following him like an extra tail.

I take off running, but I'm winded before I manage a few dozen steps. Jackie sails past me and manages to catch up with my wayward mutt, steps on his leash and brings his freedom run to an abrupt halt. Panting, he sits, as if nothing happened.

I clutch my side as I wheeze and sputter. It's so freaking embarrassing how easily I get winded. I may not be lazy, but I'm definitely out of shape. I try to mask my distress as I approach Jackie and Sparky in the next driveway.

"Thanks." I manage to speak between labored breaths.

"He's fast."

"I told you. Idiot probably saw a butterfly or something."

"You okay?"

I wipe a few beads of sweat from my forehead. I'm always sweating, even when normal people would be cold. It's simply another *lovely* aspect of being me.

I clear my throat. "Yeah, I'm fine," I lie. My lungs ache from the brief exertion, and I'm beyond mortified that I'm a gross, sweaty mess in front of Jackie. I'm *so* not okay, but I don't want to go back yet.

Thank God Jackie doesn't seem to notice what a mess I am. She picks up Sparky's leash and loops it around her wrist. "Well, lead on." She holds out her hand in a sweeping bow that makes me giggle. I try to turn it into a cough but instead I choke on my own spit.

Jackie ignores it. "I'm so ready for school to be over," she says.

"Tell me about it." I still have exams to get through, and one of them has an oral portion. I'd rather die than stand up in front of my English class where Heather and Molly can mock me relentlessly.

"Mean girls?"

"Yeah. Former best friend and her new shadow."

Jackie nods knowingly. I like that I never have to explain things to her. She just gets it.

"You a junior?"

"Sophomore, unfortunately. I can't wait to be done with this stupid town and that stupid school and all the mindless lemmings that inhabit it."

"I gotta say if I had to do another two years I might lose it," Jackie says.

"You're graduating?"

"In two weeks," she says. "With honors in case you were wondering." She glances sideways to gauge my reaction, but I'm not even a little shocked.

"That's cool. Are you going to college?"

"Eventually. But I'm paying my own way so it's either take out loans or work while I'm in school, and I'm not feeling either of those options."

I haven't considered college yet. Nothing interests me enough to spend four years studying it. But it's never been a question of whether I'll go to college, just where. It's expected. I have the grades, so college is the next step. I've already started getting postcards and catalogs from a handful of schools: a dozen or so identical brochures of sunny campuses with students lounging beneath sprawling trees, laughing at an unknown joke, biking across a quad, lugging books into a towering brick facade. I can't see myself doing any of it.

"I know what you mean," I tell her. "It all seems so pointless."

"I think if I had a specific goal in mind, it wouldn't be pointless. But I don't see why paying tens of thousands of dollars to 'find myself' is such a great idea. I'd rather bounce around Europe for a while or work on a shrimp boat for a year."

"A shrimp boat… really?"

Jackie kicks a rock that goes rolling across the sidewalk before landing in a flower bed. "Seems about as logical as choosing a random major at a random college and paying them while I figure my shit out. Why not just pick a random job? At least I'd get to see the ocean."

"Fair point."

At the park, she finds a stick for Sparky to chase. I sit on a bench and watch as she throws it and Sparky chases. Jackie becomes childlike in her glee. When Sparky finally lies down in the grass and chews on the end of the stick instead of returning it, Jackie sits down beside me and drapes her arm over the back of the bench.

"You want to catch a movie?" she asks.

Frowning, I squint into the sun. "I'm kind of broke."

"We could go to the dollar theater, and I could spot you."

I want to protest, but Jackie's hand grazes my shoulder and my brain turns to mush.

"Just say yes," Jackie pleads. "Don't make me go back to Vee's house yet." She sticks her lip out in a playful pout, and her eyes lock on mine. I can't say no with her looking at me like that.

"Okay, but I'll bring the snacks."

At first I shrug it off, chalk it up to simple admiration, but then I catch myself inching closer to catch the scent of shea butter on Jackie's skin or watching her lips as she speaks. Whenever we're together, I try to pull smiles from her, rare smiles that are saved for her closest friends. Soon the attraction becomes harder to deny. Jackie's dark eyes haunt me. I catch myself daydreaming about her smile during my trigonometry final.

"Tabitha," Mrs. Sansone whispers. "You've only got twenty minutes left."

I glance at the paper in front of me to find I've only answered three questions. Damn. I still have seventeen to go.

"Sorry," I mutter. I can't decide if I'm apologizing to her or myself.

"I can't let you in my AP calculus class unless you get at least a B on this exam," she says. The disappointment in her eyes urges me to focus.

"Sorry," I repeat. I glance behind me at the empty seat.

Mrs. Sansone pats me on the shoulder. "Everything's fine," she whispers. "Just take a deep breath and start on the next problem." Her smile is sympathetic, so I don't try to tell her that it's not the incident with Brad that's distracting me. Brad Mason was given in-school suspension for the rest of the school year. He's taking his exams in the library—far from me. And thanks to Mrs. Sansone's eye-witness report, we won't have any more classes together as long as we're at North Decker. It's a small relief, but I guess it's better than nothing.

My responding smile must convince Mrs. Sansone that I'm all right because she walks away. When she's seated at her desk, I read the next problem: "In a right triangle ABC, tan(A) = 3/4. Find sin(A) and cos(A)." Okay, I can do this. I bite my lip and work out the equation, moving through it and the next three problems in a couple of minutes. My pencil scratches across the page faster than I think I've ever written before. By the time the bell rings, I've answered all the questions and I'm reasonably sure I got the answers right for most of them. But without trig to occupy my mind, I'm back to thinking about Jackie.

It's her fault, really. She always makes me the center of attention when we're together—asking about my day, what new music I've heard, wanting to hear about my childhood. No one has ever been interested in me before. Not like that.

Meanwhile, I'd rather unravel her secrets. I want to know everything—her middle name, her hopes and dreams, her favorite food, her shoe size—everything.

She's quiet a lot, as if she's spending her time observing and reflecting rather than waiting for her turn to talk. It's tough to stare at someone when they don't speak, and I want to memorize every inch of her. So instead of last-minute cramming, I make a list of things to ask her. It takes up two pages in my notebook, front and back.

Because I'm distracted, things don't go so well during my English final. It's the one I've been dreading all week.

When it's my turn, I walk shakily to the front of the class, and Mr. Bennett reads my question aloud: "Describe the myth of the 'Self-Made Man' and explain how Thoreau's *Walden* might have reflected those values."

I clear my throat and try to put my scrambled thoughts into words. I'd only read half of the book before giving up and throwing it under my bed. The sentences went on for entire paragraphs. Whole chapters were bloated asides about bugs or solitude or some other nonsense. How could anyone read that thing? I try not to look at Heather, but I can hear her whispering to Molly.

"Miss Davidson, quiet please," says Mr. Bennett.

I finish my rambling soliloquy and take my seat. Heather snickers, and Molly stage-whispers. "You've got a booger hanging out of your nose."

I reach up before my brain catches up with my actions. There's nothing there, but by the time I realize it, Heather and Molly are giggling so hard, Mr. Bennett has to smack a paperweight on his desk to shut them up.

"If you two can't be quiet, I'm docking you each one letter grade on your final."

Heather's laughter sputters to a halt but Molly is shaking as she tries to control hers. I'm so glad to be finished with this school year. When the bell rings, I practically run down the hall and into the overcast afternoon.

I cut through the 7-Eleven parking lot because it's shorter and I don't want to get caught in the rain. Unfortunately, Mike is a creature of habit and he's still smoking his menthols behind the dumpster. When he sees me, he smiles and waves.

"Look what the cat dragged in," he says.

I can tell he's trying to sound tough but I can see in his eyes he's actually excited to see me. So much for caring the least. Even though I'm over my misguided crush, I can't help the feeling of butterflies in my gut as I walk toward him. I square my shoulders and try to act normal.

"I can't stay," I tell him.

His face falls. "Not even for old time's sake?"

"Sorry. I—" His defeated expression makes me stop mid-sentence. I look up at the gray sky and consider the odds that I can still beat the rain home. "I suppose I could stay for a few minutes."

Triumphant, he lights a second cigarette and hands it to me.

"I'd given up on you," he says with a wink.

"Yeah, I guess I've been… busy." I take a reluctant drag on the cigarette, and it makes me cough. I drop it on the ground and stub it out.

Mike's jaw drops. "Jesus, Tabitha, don't waste my smokes."

"Sorry," I snap. "But it's not like I *asked* for it. You just handed it to me."

"It's called a friendly gesture," Mike says. "But maybe you forgot that we're friends."

"I didn't forget. But I think you did when you tried to kiss me."

I'm not even sure it *was* an attempt. But the sour taste his comment left was reminiscent of the stunt Brad pulled. They both felt like violations. As if someone had changed the rules without telling me. My stomach rolls as I swallow back bile. The nausea only lasts for a moment, but as soon as it wanes, I want to go the fuck home, and stupid Mike is standing in my way. "Move," I demand through clenched teeth.

He stands firm. "Who pissed on your corn flakes this morning? I don't see you for weeks and you finally show up and you're a total…" Mike's lip curls in disgust. "Bitch."

I glare at him and clench my hands into fists. I want to punch him. He's never called a girl a bitch, and now he chooses to direct it at me? I know if I stay I'm going to do something I can't take back, so I turn and stomp through the parking lot.

Mike calls after me, "I'm sorry! Tabitha, come back. I'm sorry!"

I feel hot tears on my cheeks, but I'm angry, not sad. "Fuck off!" I shout. And as I give him an angry salute with my middle finger, the tears turn into a cheek-splitting smile. My first thought is, "I have to tell Jackie."

CHUBBY BUNNY NO. 1

Dear jerk on the corner cat-calling yet another grrrl,

We don't owe you anything because girls don't owe guys a minute of their time. It's OUR choice if we want to talk to you or kiss you or have sex with you. OUR choice. Not yours. I am so sick and tired of guys thinking that women are their property just because we exist. Hundreds of years of history of men subjugating women and all I can think of is flipping you off. All of you. You take our innocence and femininity and chew it up and spit it out. Sometimes under the guise of friendship. Sometimes under the mantra of "you just need a man."

I am sick and tired of this bullshit. I am fed up. I think from now on I'm only going to date girls because all the guys I know are fuckups and assholes. I'm sorry, they just are. Maybe all guys aren't like that, but in my experience, they're just not worth the hassle.

My friend Jackie is a lesbian. (Don't worry. I got her permission to say that... I'd never out a friend). She doesn't dress to entice the male gaze. She's butch. She's proud. I want to be more like her. I want to not care what people think. I want to scream from the rooftops that I LIKE GIRLS!

That doesn't mean I hate guys, but I gotta tell you, if guys don't start shaping up, I might just have to start.

Sincerely and with much anger,

Tabitha

~~PS: I secretly wish I'd get cat-called even though I know it's misogynistic. I worry that makes me a bad feminist. But sometimes being fat is just depressing and I want to be noticed and called pretty. I hate that I feel that way. I hate that society has made me feel that way. Don't cat-call me. But maybe do.~~

FAT GIRLS HAVE FEELINGS TOO

I eat.
I sleep.
I dream.
I wake.
I'm fat.

She eats.
She sleeps.
She dreams.
She wakes.
She's thin.

We are both human beings.
We have breasts and stomachs and legs and hundreds of other parts in common.
We have to eat to live.
But all you see is size.

And you tell me:
I'm fat because I'm lazy.
I'm fat because I eat too much.
I'm fat because I don't care about my appearance.

Well, fuck you.
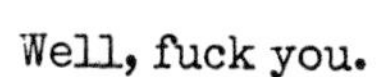
We're both beautiful.
And we don't need you anyway.

CHAPTER 8

"MONIQUE DOESN'T THINK WE SHOULD go to the Riot Grrrl meetings anymore."

Jackie and I are lying on my bed watching TV when she drops this bombshell.

"You can't," I say, realizing as the words leave my lips how much like a child I sound.

"I think you guys talk about important stuff, but it's just not our thing, man." Jackie has one slender arm behind her head and is staring at my ceiling. I can't read her expression.

"What do you mean?" I ask, muting the TV.

She rolls on her side, and I can see in her eyes that she's serious. "Y'all mean well, but I can't ignore that me, Venus and Monique are the only black girls there. And it's not just you guys. The whole damn scene is so white. Did you see the crowd at Spring Fest? If you don't count Venus and Cherie, who were onstage for all of ten minutes, I was the only non-white person there."

"That's just Decker," I say. "There's not a lot of diversity, but it's not like we're all racist or anything."

Jackie laughs, but I don't understand what is so funny.

"You're cute, Tabitha, but incredibly naïve." She taps the tip of my nose with her index finger.

"I'm cute?" I say. I choose to ignore the naïve part, especially because I still don't know why she thinks what I said is funny. I'd rather encourage the flirtatious glint in her eyes than decipher her meaning.

Jackie turns away from me and grabs a pillow. She hits me with it; it's a light tap, with no force behind it. It's playful. Her laughter is loud and boisterous, nothing like my bumbling, donkey-like guffaw. How could she possibly think I'm cute? She's just being nice.

Jackie stops mid-swipe with her pillow and asks, "Hey, do you want to go to Great America with me and Venus next weekend after graduation?"

"Great America? With you? Uh…" I stand there staring at her as if I've been struck dumb. Does she really mean it? I close my mouth to keep from looking like a deranged goldfish.

"You know, Six Flags…" She grins and tosses the pillow in the air. "Roller coasters…" She catches it and then flies it around my room the way my mom used to do with a spoonful of peas when I refused to eat. "We can ride the Demon until we puke." She mimics a barfing noise and doubles over in mock pain. "Then we'll ride some other shit until we've recovered enough to do that old wooden one. You know the big, scary one with two tracks?"

"I don't know," I say, trying to hide my smirk. "Sounds pretty boring to me."

Jackie stops her theatrics and stares at me. "Boring? Are you crazy?"

"Gotcha," I say as my pillow makes contact with her face.

As I erupt into giggles, she tackles me to the bed and wallops me with her pillow. I cover my face with my hands to deflect the blows, though they don't hurt.

"What in heaven's name is going on in here?"

I crack open one eye to see my mom standing in the doorway. She looks pissed.

I sit up, and Jackie jumps down from the bed. "Jackie and I were just goofing around, Mom." I try to smooth my hair down, but it's no use. We worked up some static during the pillow fight, and my mousy brown hair is standing on end.

Jackie snorts as she tries to hold in a laugh, which sends me into a fit of giggles. We give each other sidelong glances, and Jackie winks at me. My heart races; I almost forget Mom's in the room. My face is stuck in a big, goofy grin.

My mom clears her throat. "I've ordered some takeout," she says. "I didn't know you had a friend over, but there's probably enough."

"You want to stay for dinner?" I ask.

Jackie looks from me to my mom and back to me. "Are you sure?"

"As long as you don't try to make it sound like you're murdering Tabitha during dinner," Mom says. She laughs when we both look at her. "You two were screaming bloody murder up here. I thought someone had broken in."

"Nobody here but us queers," I say with a laugh. I can feel Jackie's eyes on me, but I simply smile at my mom. "We'll be down in a minute."

"I'm going to get changed. Can you girls set the table?"

"Sure thing, Mom."

When she's gone, Jackie looks at me in wonderment. "Your mom knows you're bi?"

"I'm pretty sure she thinks I'm a lesbian, but yeah. She figured it out when I was 'going out' with Kate." I use air quotes around "going out," but if Jackie notices, she doesn't react.

"And she doesn't care?"

"I'm sure she'd prefer it if I were straight, but she hasn't disowned me or anything. We don't really talk about it."

Jackie scrubs a hand across her face.

"What about you?" I ask. "Does your family know?"

She sucks in a sharp breath and nods grimly. "Yeah, they know."

"And?"

Jackie scoffs. "Well, there's a reason I'm sleeping on Vee's couch and it's not because I like those hideous orange throw pillows."

"Your parents kicked you out?" I can't imagine anyone being able to throw their son or daughter out on the street. My mom may not be perfect, but she'd never kick me out for something I have no control over.

"More or less."

"God, Jack, that's awful." I reach for her hand, but she pulls away. Tears pool around her dark eyes and wet her long lashes.

"I'll live," she says. "I don't need that kind of shit in my life."

Now I know where Jackie's tough façade comes from. And I don't blame her.

I stand and throw my arm around her. "Why don't we go downstairs and drown our sorrows in whatever junk food my mom has waiting for us? And then on Sunday, we'll ride roller coasters until we puke. Think you can handle that?"

She smiles at me and wipes away a lone tear. "Oh, I can handle it. The question is, can you?"

"Ten bucks says you scream louder than me on the first drop."

"Deal."

We shake on it and go downstairs.

On a roller coaster, the first hill is always the biggest, and it's kind of like that with Jackie, too. After she tells me about her mom, she opens up more. We tell each other our secrets and laugh at private jokes. We mostly hang at my house, but sometimes we sit on her "bed" at Venus's house and watch cheesy horror movies. Jackie likes the buckets of fake blood. I'm more a fan of the bad acting.

"Oh, come on! Don't go down the stairs!" Jackie gestures toward the TV as if she's trying to make sure I'm watching.

I roll my eyes, but I love it when she shouts at the TV. We throw popcorn at the screen when the movie ends badly. It's easy being with Jackie.

When the tape ends and we're left with static, the screen lights our faces eerily and flickers tentatively in the shadows.

"Janae would have loved that movie," Jackie says quietly.

"Who's Janae?"

"My baby sister." Jackie pauses and takes a deep breath. "I missed her birthday."

I place my hand on Jackie's shoulder and wait until she looks like she can speak without crying. "How old is she?"

Jackie attempts a smile. "She just turned twelve."

"Rough age." I remember being twelve. Even though Heather and I were still friends back then, I struggled to feel that I belonged, and puberty had given me boobs overnight. Suddenly I didn't look like the other girls, and everyone took notice. Was Jackie's experience similar? "You really miss her, huh?"

Jackie nods. "Leaving Janae was the worst part about moving out. That little girl followed me everywhere—just like a puppy. I used to hate it, but now I wonder all the time what she's up to. Who's she following around now?" Jackie sighs. "Sometimes I call the house and hope she answers just so I can hear her voice."

"Have you talked to her?"

Jackie's eyes glisten. "No. Jerome usually answers the phone, and he won't tell her that I called."

"Is that your brother?"

She nods. "He's fifteen and he—" Jackie cuts herself off with a sob. "Shit. I hate crying."

I rub comforting circles on her back—at least I hope it's comforting. We've never established what kind of touching is okay. "You don't have to tell me if you don't want to."

"I know I don't, but I want to. Just give me a minute."

I sit back against the outdated velvet throw pillows and wait. Jackie seems to be working up to something.

"I told you about my mom, but I didn't tell you the whole story. She didn't kick me out, not really."

"But you said—"

She shakes her head. "You assumed. I never corrected you."

I'm embarrassed, but I try not to let it show. How could I be so dumb, assuming things about Jackie yet again? I take a calming breath and ask, "Okay, so what *did* happen?"

"When I came out, Mom wasn't surprised. I think she kind of knew. I mean, look at me." Jackie gestures at her faded jeans and her short hair. "I dress like a dude; I cut my hair like a dude." She takes a steadying breath. "But she didn't really say much. Jerome, though, he just kept picking and picking and picking. At first I thought he was just giving me shit, you know? But then a guy from school started yelling stuff at me about how I was a dyke and was going to hell; Jerome just stood there and let it happen. He didn't say anything. And when I told the principal about what had happened, Jerome said I made the whole thing up."

"What an asshole."

Jackie's lips quirk into a half smile that fades as quickly as it appears. "Hey, he's still family."

"Family or not, he has no right to treat you that way."

Jackie shrugs. "Anyway, I was eighteen already so I moved out. Vee's parents let me crash here."

Her response is so nonchalant, it's as if she's just told me she's having pizza for dinner. I can't imagine living near my mom and not talking to her. How can Jackie be okay with this? Tentatively, I lay my hand on top of hers. "What about the rest of your family?"

"My baby brother, Jackson, doesn't really understand, and I think Mom was hurt that I moved out, but Jerome just dumped all my clothes in the front yard."

"Jack, that's awful." I grip her hand tightly and she squeezes back. We're silent for a while, letting the white noise of the VCR lull us into half-sleep.

"Jack?"

"Hmm?"

"I'm glad you told me."

"Me too."

"Can I ask you one thing?"

Jackie turns her head so she's facing me and nods.

"What's your mom's name?" I ask.

She raises a single eyebrow at me. "Deborah. Why?"

"Not Judy or Janet… or maybe Justine?"

"Shut up." She swats at my arm and then sighs. "I know, it's dumb. She gave us all names that start with J. She always liked the name Jacqueline and I think it sort of got out of hand after that."

"So your dad's not a Jason or a Jeremiah?"

She rolls her eyes, but I know she's not mad at me because she's grinning. She gets up to switch out the tape out for the next movie.

"It's not dumb. I like that you all have 'J' names."

"It *is* dumb. And I thought you would be on my side, since you were named after a cheesy TV witch."

She flings herself at the couch but manages to land softly—like a dancer. Of course, when I nudge her with my knee, it jostles the popcorn bowl. Completely *anti*-graceful. The few kernels in the bottom skitter around before coming to rest again. That's how I feel talking to Jackie. Gentle nudges followed by random loops and spins before we settle into quiet comfort again.

"I think I would like it more if there were more 'witches' in the family," I say. "If I had an Uncle Arthur, or if my dad's name was Darrin. Then it would make sense."

She picks through the bowl for the half-popped kernels. "No it wouldn't."

She's right. It's kind of cheesy no matter how you look at it. "At least you have company in your misery," I say.

"It's not all it's cracked up to be." Jackie stands; I take it as an indication that this line of conversation is over. "You want more popcorn before we start the next one?"

"Sure," I say.

Jackie pauses on her way to the kitchen. "Tabitha, would you like to go to my graduation tomorrow?"

"I'd be honored."

JACKIE'S MOM SHOWS UP ALONE to her graduation, and afterward they step away to talk. Jackie doesn't bring up their conversation, so I don't. Instead I focus on our road trip to Six Flags. I made a mix tape for the ride and I'm excited for Jackie to hear it.

Marty somehow managed to get herself invited on our trip, so I'm stuffed into the back seat of Jackie's car with her. The radio got turned down ten minutes ago when Marty kept shouting over it.

"All I'm saying is, we could talk about how black girls are treated differently than white girls," Venus says from the front seat.

"But we're *all* harassed," Marty says, leaning forward over the center console. "We're all girls. Why should race make any difference?"

"See, that shit right there is what I'm talking about," Venus says, throwing up her hands in exasperation. "A black woman shares her experience and y'all act like it's not valid because you've never experienced it."

"I've never seen it happen," Marty says.

"I'm *telling* you it happens," Venus says.

"This is going nowhere," Marty replies. She sighs and slams her body against the seat.

"Only because you're not listening," Jackie says. "If you'd ever shut the hell up for five minutes, you might actually learn something."

"I'm listening," Marty says. "I just think you're blowing this race thing out of proportion. Why does it always have to be about race?"

Venus turns around in her seat, and if looks could kill, Marty would be the deadest of the dead. "This 'race thing'? Do you even listen to yourself?"

"I don't see color," Marty says. "I see people."

Venus turns to Jackie. "Would it be considered self-defense if I kill a white bitch for being ignorant as hell?"

Marty looks at me as if she wants me to back her up, but I'm not sure what to say. Maybe Venus is right. I grew up in Decker, where it's front-page news whenever a black person moves to town. How can I possibly know what it's like for them?

"I think what my esteemed colleague here is trying to say," Jackie says, "is that it's also racist to say you 'don't see color.'"

Marty bristles. She always *has* to be right, and even if she eventually agrees with someone, she won't admit it.

"I don't get it," I say. "I thought that was the whole point—*not* to see color."

"Not exactly," Jackie says. "It's like saying you're ignoring the fact that we are black. You *see* that we're black and that affects how you perceive us, even if you think it doesn't. When you ignore our color, you ignore our struggles."

"Oh my God," Marty says. "Segregation ended, like what, thirty years ago?"

"Ugh, that is so not the point," Venus says. "You know what? I think it's best if we don't talk any more. We're going to celebrate my girl Jackie's graduation, and I'm not going to let you ruin it, Marty."

"But—"

Venus holds up a hand. "Shut it."

I grab Marty's arm. "Just let it go, okay. This trip is supposed to be fun."

I catch Jackie's eye in the rearview, and she mouths, "Thank you." I'm not sure what she's thanking me for, but I mouth, "You're welcome," anyway.

Venus turns up the radio, and Marty pouts the rest of the way to Gurnee.

WE'RE IN LINE FOR A giant wooden rollercoaster when Jackie kisses me. It's only a peck on the cheek, but it sends shivers through me all the same.

"What was that for?" I ask.

"Just for being you. For coming to my graduation and for shutting Marty the hell up."

I blush. I feel it without having to see my round cheeks turn bright red. Sometimes, I swear I'd like to invent a time machine so I can go back and make sure my Irish grandmother never meets my grandfather. But then I guess I wouldn't be here. And I also wouldn't be standing under a sign that says "Your wait time from this point is 60 minutes" blushing like an idiot.

Jackie drops her head and rubs the back of her neck. She's nervous, too. I reach for her arm, careful to make it as platonic as possible, and she meets my gaze.

"Are we...?" I stop myself. What if she rejects me? What if someone sees us?

"I'd like to be," Jackie says, her voice wavering. "If that's what you want."

I can't stop the smile that breaks out so I don't even try. "Yeah, I'd like that." I resist the urge to throw my arms around her neck and pull her to me.

Jackie must be bolder than me, because she looks around to make sure no one's looking at us and then threads her hand through mine. She tugs me closer and hides our twined fingers behind my leg, but still. It feels good. I'm holding hands in public with my girlfriend.

My heart might burst from my chest. For more than one reason.

DECKED OUT NO. 6

MY FEMINISM IS FOR ME—IS THAT OKAY?

BY KATE GOLDBERG

I thought that maybe being active in social causes was the best thing I could do to forward the cause of women and girls. What I failed to notice was being too active can blind you to protecting the real women and girls in your life.

I think I screwed up big time. I broke a girl's heart and worse still it was because of a guy. Does that make me a bad feminist?

I wear red lipstick and expensive perfume. I kiss girls and boys. I drink coffee and beer and eat meat. Do those things make me a bad feminist?

I wonder all the time about the things that define us and what they really mean about our feminism and our rage. Is it okay to be angry all the time if it's in self-defense? Or should I try to be careful with others' feelings even if they might hurt me? I was raised to be compassionate and empathetic, but do those things fly in the face of modern feminism? Should I be as bumbling and unapologetic as a man? I'm a woman. What if I want to BE a woman? What does it mean to be a woman?

Am I a woman simply because I was slapped on the ass at birth and given a pink blanket? Isn't there more to it than that?

Where is the "woman" threshold? Is it an age? A developmental stage? A mindset?

Am I me if I dress like a man? If I wear pants and neckties and combat boots do I cease to be feminine? Why should someone else get to dictate my gender or my style? Why can't I shave my head and call it a day? For once I'd like to throw on sloppy clothes and a baseball cap and only worry about trying to get laid.

Who made these rules? And why do I feel like I have to follow them even when I know I shouldn't?

CHAPTER 9

WITH SUMMER IN FULL SWING, Jackie and I have nothing to do so we hang out with each other as much as possible. In many ways, it's a lot like being with Kate. But in other ways—the important ways—it's totally different. Kate spent her time educating me and asking me to champion her causes. Jackie spends her time getting to know me and asking me what I'd like to do. Mostly I want to be with Jackie.

I spend lazy afternoons wrapped in her arms as we talk about our dreams for the future. We lay out in my backyard in our bathing suits until our skin burns—mine cherry red, hers a deep, earthy brown. We dance in my room with the music cranked as loud as it will go. We walk hand in hand to Riot Grrrl meetings and cuddle while Shut Up practices their set. While waiting in line for the movies, we stand as close as we dare without being noticed. We go shopping together and make out in the Sears dressing room with discarded jeans and dresses at our feet. We giggle until our faces ache. We discover our bodies and our hearts. We fall in love. Or at least I do.

"I wish I had the balls to cut my hair that short," I tell Jackie for the hundredth time. She's sitting on my bed reading the liner notes from a CD she brought over. I've never heard of the group, but the music—an eclectic mix of rap and punk—is growing on me. When she looks up, her soft smile is the same as it has been every time I've said the same thing. She strokes my hair gently and tucks a strand behind my ear. "I like your hair," she says. "It's soft. Gives me something to play with when we make out."

I shrug but lean into her touch. "Maybe I'm jealous of your shower-and-go look."

Her responding smirk is flirtatious and seductive. "Or maybe you like really butch chicks."

"Stop, you're not butch." I lean in for a kiss.

Jackie sits up straighter, and her smile fades. She pulls away from my touch. "It's not a dirty word, Tabitha. I'm proud of it."

"I know you are, honey, but I don't see it the way you do." To emphasize my point, I brush her breast with the back of my hand. It's just a tease, and I hope it leads to more. "You're all woman to me," I whisper.

She pushes my hand away, and I stare at it in shock. "Jacks—"

"Tabitha, just because someone is more masculine doesn't mean she's not a woman. There's more to me than what I look like. You should understand that better than anyone."

That hurts. She knows I'm self-conscious about my weight. We've talked about it, but she's never mentioned it before, not like this.

"I know that… It's just—" I cut myself off because I'm trying not to cry and also I don't want to fight with Jackie. "I think you're beautiful and I like that you're a girl. I know you like being butch, but the world doesn't accept butch girls."

"I don't give a fuck about the rest of the world," Jackie says. "And I can't believe you're saying this. Since when do you care who accepts us?" Her eyes narrow, and the heat from her judgment burns me.

"Look, I'm sorry I said anything." Trying to coax back her smile, I stroke her cheek and press a soft kiss to her lips. "I don't care who accepts us. I want you to know *I* accept you."

"Well, I'm butch. I've even been known to call myself a dyke." She raises an eyebrow. "You're going to have to get used to it."

"I'm used to it," I say, peppering her cheeks with soft kisses between words. "In fact, I'm quite a fan."

She sinks into my touch, but then shakes her head as if to clear it. "You can't just kiss me every time we disagree."

"Try me," I say as I push closer, teasing her lips with my tongue. When her lips part, I know our argument is over.

LATER, WHEN OUR LIPS ARE sore and there's nowhere else to go but further, which neither of us is ready for, we decide to take a break. Jackie lies on my bed with her right arm bent behind her head, and I tuck my head between her left shoulder and elbow to sling my leg over hers. It's a little too warm to snuggle—my cheek sticks to Jackie's arm—but neither of us seems to care as we lie there. My eyes drift closed as I listen to Jackie's even, slow breaths. I'm nearly lulled to sleep by the rhythm.

"What are you thinking?" I say after a bit, still half asleep and completely blissed out.

"About what you said earlier."

I open my eyes with sudden alertness, but all I can see is the edge of Jackie's jaw. I can't read her expression. I crane my neck a little to try to see her face. "Are we okay?"

She angles her chin so we can make eye contact. "I'm not angry, Tabitha," she says. "I just want you to like me for me."

I prop myself up on my elbow and look down at her. Her eyes are wide and watery, and her lips form a tentative smile. There is a vulnerability in her expression I've never seen before. So I let her words sit with me. I remember feeling that way with Kate. That maybe who I was wasn't the person she wanted to be with. That she was trying to mold me into someone she *could* love. It hurts. And the truth is, I love everything about Jackie. I don't want her to change.

"I do. I wouldn't change a thing."

I feel, rather than hear, her breath catch, and she freezes for a second before relaxing into me. Jackie's fingers trace a gentle path down my back and I close my eyes to savor it, again resting my head on her chest.

"I can't believe I'm with you," Jackie says. "I walked in that rec center and there you were, looking like a dazed feral cat, hanging on Kate Goldberg's every word. I thought you were some kind of groupie."

I laugh. "Me? A groupie?"

"Okay, I have a confession."

I lift my head.

"Riot Grrrl wasn't the first place I saw you," she says.

Intrigued, I pull myself to a sitting position. I cross my arms over my chest and wait. "Yeah?"

Jackie scoots up toward the headboard until she's sitting facing me. "It was that Bikini Kill show a few months back, remember?"

I remember the concert, but I don't remember Jackie. Could she really have been there watching me? Could I have been that oblivious? "Really?"

Jackie nods. "I saw you the minute you walked in. I thought you were cute with your humongous black boots and messy hair. You were with some guy, and you both looked bored by the opening band. So you went to the merch table. You were so shy and nervous. I tried to say hi, but you were busy talking to Kate. So I stood back and waited, but I lost you in the crowd. And then later, I noticed you down front but you were arm in arm with some redheaded girl. I saw the way you looked at her, and I knew you had to be… well, I thought you were gay but—"

"You weren't far off."

"Right."

"So was Riot Grrrl a coincidence then?"

Jackie drops her chin to her chest and covers her face with her hand. "Not exactly."

I pull her hand away. "Stalker," I tease.

She's blushing and trying to hide her smile. It's sweet.

"I couldn't help it. I had such a crush from the first moment I saw you."

"Me? Really?" As much as I know that Jackie is into me, I still have a hard time believing that she'd pick me over someone as dynamic as Kate or as petite and feminine as Cherie or as outspoken as Marty. Next to them I feel like an old shoe—a favorite, comfortable shoe, but still a shoe.

"Yes, you," she says. "You've got such a great smile and you aren't always trying to get people to notice you."

"No, I'm usually trying to disappear."

"But you stand out. You're beautiful."

I wave her off and duck behind my hair.

"No, really," she says, leaning into my sight line. "You have the sweetest little nose, and the prettiest gray-blue eyes. And you're so…" She bites her lip and gives me a seductive once-over. "Sexy."

Now she's teasing. "Stop."

"I'm serious."

"But I'm so…" Hideous. Gargantuan. Ugly. Stupid. Lazy. A whale. Flabby Tabby. At least a hundred words fly through my mind in mere seconds, but what I say is, "Fat."

Jackie smirks. "I'd say 'thick,' and it's one of my favorite things about you."

It's the first time in my life I've ever considered that someone might find my body type attractive. My thighs chafe if I wear a skirt. I get heat rash under my arms if my sleeves are too loose. There are rolls of fat on my front *and* back. Whenever I sit down, I have to move the button on my jeans so it doesn't poke me in the bellybutton. There's nothing attractive about any of it. I've thought someday someone might find me attractive in spite of my size, but not *because* of it. In this moment, staring at Jackie as she tells me I'm beautiful, I feel my heart practically pound out of my chest. I can't form words.

"I know it's not what is usually considered attractive," Jackie says, ducking her head shyly. "But I've never been one to follow the crowd."

"I–" How do I form sounds into meaningful phrases? "You—"

After I force out a few more single-syllable noises, Jackie places her hand over mine. "You're really shocked, aren't you?" The teasing light in Jackie's eyes gives way to something more serious. "Tabitha, hasn't anyone ever told you you're beautiful?"

I try to think. I'm sure my mom has called me cute… pretty even. But beautiful? I don't think that word has ever been uttered in my presence to describe even a piece of me. I've heard it lobbed at models and actresses, Heather and even Molly. My mother has been described as unconventionally beautiful. I've gotten the occasional, "Your hair looks nice like that." But not *me*. Never the whole of me. I'm just Tabitha. I'm like a muted wallpaper—something to blend into the background and not meant to be noticed. I'm here but I add nothing to the world—a mix of color and pattern with no discernible purpose.

"Do you ever feel so insignificant you wonder if you're even real?" The words flow from me like a tide, bubbling up and over before ebbing in a hushed whisper.

"You're not insignificant." Jackie's eyes are wide and fixed on mine. "And you're *so* real."

"But you know what I mean?" I choke on a sob. "All my life I've felt like I'm floating. Like I'm waiting to feel what everyone else feels."

"And what does everyone else feel?"

The word catches in my throat. A giant lump of truth that won't budge. I swallow around cotton. "Human," I rasp.

"And you? You're not human?" Her hand caresses mine, but I'm detached from it.

"I'm—" I pause and close my eyes. I take a steadying breath. Once I admit this, she'll know, and that could be it for us. Whatever she thinks of me in this moment could change everything. "I'm… such a loser. I act like I know what I'm doing, but honestly, I haven't got a clue. And I'm afraid that if I ever show any sign of weakness everyone will know that I'm only pretending!" I cry into my sweaty palm, too ashamed to look Jackie in the face.

A broken laugh pulls my attention back. This is it. Jackie thinks I'm a giant moron who can't get through a day of school without feeling helpless. I brace myself for the inevitable. I peek through my fingers to find Jackie gazing back at me with a half-smile on her lips and tenderness in her eyes.

"Tabitha, everyone feels that way."

"Everyone?"

Jackie's eyes trail skyward. "Well, maybe not *everyone* everyone, but plenty of people. Me, for example."

"You? But you're so confident all the time."

"Look, I'm just trying to fake it till I make it. Just like the rest of the world."

"No, Heather, Kate, Marty for crying out loud! They're all so confident and outspoken."

"Do you really think that Heather chick is mean to you because she's confident? Or that Marty never shuts up because she thinks she has something valuable to say? And Kate? Really? With all the causes and shit, I thought you knew she was compensating for something."

I can't seem to do anything but blink. Jackie's words have met my ears but their meaning hasn't yet made its way to my addled brain. All those girls I look up to, they're just as scared shitless as I am? I picture Marty on her bed at night writing her woes into a journal, pouring her heart into its pages. Kate, searching a magazine for causes that are "cool." She picks one that some famous singer champions. Last is Heather. She stands in front of a mirror scrutinizing her body more harshly than she's ever judged mine. She pinches her side so hard it hurts. She wishes the inches away.

In one surreal moment, it all makes sense. I look at Jackie, who has just bared her soul to me. She had a crush on me and took a chance. She had no way of knowing I'd feel the same way. We're all the same. I'm normal.

An unbidden laugh bubbles up and then another. I snort. Pretty soon I'm laughing so hard I can't see.

Jackie's brow furrows in confusion. "What's so funny?"

I want to tell her how I had been terrified she'd break up with me because I'm such a loser. How I thought I was the only person on the planet who wanted to disappear. To hide. I want to tell her I'm laughing because I was so afraid I was a freak that I failed to notice how completely ordinary I am. That in my quest to blend, I have achieved ultimate chameleon status. I'm *literally* just like everyone else.

But I can't speak. I'm laughing so hard I've started crying again and now Jackie is giggling too. When we finally manage to calm down, I'm out of breath. Jackie strokes my arm until my chest stops heaving and I can speak.

I swipe at a stray tear. "God, I feel like an idiot."

"Welcome to the club." She holds out her arms and I fold into them, letting her warmth envelop me.

I'm home.

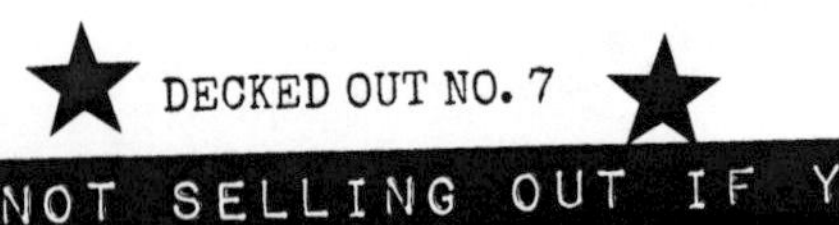

DECKED OUT NO. 7

IT'S NOT SELLING OUT IF YOU SLEEP IN THE VAN!

OH MY GRAVY, our band Shut Up is going on tour! I can hardly believe it. We're like a real band and everything now!!!! It's only a few shows and we're playing with two other bands, and most of the gigs are in seedy little dives that I wouldn't normally be caught dead in, but these are real, paying gigs. Well, if we can get people to show up. So that's where you come in.

Everyone, load into vans, hatchbacks, trucks, station wagons, your mom's minivan, whatever you've got and get your butt to one of these shows. More if you can. I promise we'll rock. These are all-ages shows, so bring your little sisters.

And to sweeten the deal, here are the lyrics to our next original song.

xoxo
Cherie

BITE ME (LYRICS)

by Marty DeVane and Cherie Wong

It takes a big man to tell a girl no
It takes a hot girl to put on a show
I wanna take you home
I wanna get you alone
But if you want to be with me there's one thing to know

If it ain't broke, don't fix it
If it's all right I'll say so
But if it ain't on the menu you're leaving hungry
And I got news for you, you'll have to go

Bite me
(Bite me yeah!)
Bite me
(Bite me yeah!)

I'm the one who makes the rules
And there's nothing you can do so
Bite me!

You'll need a bottle for your baby
You'll need a leash for your dog
But since I'm neither one, boy, just move it along
And I got news for you, you'll have to go

Bite me
(Bite me yeah!)
Bite me
(Bite me yeah!)
I'm the one who makes the rules
And there's nothing you can do so
Bite me!

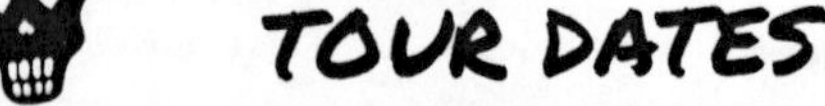

JULY 7 - AURORA, IL AT THE PIT

JULY 8 - ROCKFORD, IL AT VORTEX

JULY 9 - MADISON, WI AT RED SQUARE

JULY 10 - MILWAUKEE, WI AT ANNE & FRANKS

JULY 13 - DUBUQUE, IA AT THE RESISTANCE

JULY 14 - PEORIA, IL AT THE CHERRY BOMB

JULY 15 - CHAMPAIGN, IL AT THE STRAY CAT

JULY 16 - TERRE HAUTE, IN AT WINKIES (18+ only... sorry, this couldn't be helped)

JULY 17 - INDIANAPOLIS AT THE MOTORHEAD LOUNGE

JULY 21 - SOUTH BEND, IN AT LUCKY PENNY'S

JULY 22 - GARY, IN AT THE STARLIGHT CANTINA

JULY 23 - CHICAGO AT THE MOLOTOV BALLROOM

CHAPTER 10

"And then she says, 'So, Tabitha, tell me about a time when you were faced with a challenge and how you overcame it.'"

"Again? Ugh! Why do they always ask that question?" Cherie rolls her eyes as I recount my interview experience. I had asked her to help me find something to wear to the interview so I'd promised a full recap.

"No clue, but it's like it's a prerequisite or something. I swear they all ask the same stupid questions."

This was my third interview at the mall and the third time I'd been asked a variation of this question. The first time I bumbled through something about how I didn't get a bike for my seventh birthday and how I cried to my mom until my grandpa got me a pink banana-seated wonder. Of course they never called me back, so for the second interview I talked about my struggle with chemistry and how I buckled down and applied myself until I brought my C up to a B. I got called back for a second interview but didn't get the job. "I don't know, but this time I came prepared."

"So what did you say?"

"Well, I started with something like, 'To be honest, I thrive on challenges. I think you can often learn more from failure than you can success, so I try to learn as much as I can from all my experiences.'"

"Nice."

"Then I gave them some story my mom helped me make up. I asked her what she would say to that question, and she helped me craft something simple but meaningful."

Cherie grins broadly. "Well, it worked… You got the job!"

"I got the job. Starting Saturday, I'm the newest sales associate at The Place, an 'upscale clothing boutique' for people with too much money and no thighs. It pays barely above minimum wage and I have to start out manning the fitting rooms and folding T-shirts, but it gets me off the couch and, more importantly, it means I'll have spending money for hanging with Jackie."

"That's faboo," Cherie says. "So does that mean you'll miss opening night of our tour?"

"Not a chance. I already asked for that night off. Jackie and I will be there front row, center, and dancing our faces off."

"I'm so nervous," Cherie confides. She lowers her head, and her shiny hair falls in her face. "I keep thinking I'm going to hit a wrong note or something."

"You're going to do great," I say, trying to sound as reassuring as possible. "How many songs do you have now?"

"I think we have three that we can play without messing up. Plus the covers. We should have a few more by the time the tour starts."

"Why don't you guys do a dress rehearsal? I'm sure we can secure the rec center for another hour after Tuesday's Riot Grrrl meeting."

"That's not a bad idea. I'll have to see if Kate's free. She probably has some sort of protest or rally that night." Cherie rolls her eyes, but I can tell she's exaggerating for my benefit.

I pick at the edge of Cherie's bedspread. "So, uh… how is Kate?"

Cherie half-smiles and shrugs. "She's Kate, you know. Always off on another cause, kind of oblivious to everyone around her."

"Yeah."

"She misses you, though."

"Really?"

"Yeah. She told me the other day she wished you hadn't been a casualty of her 'exploration of her sexuality' or whatever." Cherie sighs and looks at me knowingly. "I think she'd say sorry if you talked to her."

"Maybe. I'm not sure I'm ready."

I know I'm over Kate. My heart is completely tied up in Jackie, but I don't know if I can handle the awkwardness of talking with my ex. Kate broke my heart, and it's only now that I'm getting the pieces back in the right place. What if she undoes all my hard work?

"I get it," Cherie says. "I just wanted you to know that she feels awful. She didn't mean to fuck up your friendship."

"I know," I say. And I mean it. Kate is one of those people who can get so caught up in the thrill of the moment that they don't realize they were the hurricane at the center of it all until they see the destruction at their feet. It's part of what makes her so intriguing, and I can't fault her for being exciting. It's what attracted me to her in the first place. "Kate's unique."

"That's putting it mildly," Cherie jokes. "So what's going on with you and Jackie? Everything good there?"

I nod and can't keep a smile from splitting my cheeks. "She's amazing. The absolute sweetest person I've ever met, and she always wants to know what I think. It's kind of refreshing after Kate bulldozing me with her own opinions."

"Girl, I know exactly what you mean. Between Marty, Kate and Venus, I never get a word in edgewise. I'm kind of afraid to tell them I've sort of been seeing someone."

"Who?" I bounce on Cherie's bed, knocking the headboard against the wall. "Sorry." I blush hot as I realize my weight nearly put a hole in her wall.

"It's okay, the frame's busted on this side. I do it all the time."

I can't tell if she's saving my feelings or telling the truth. So I steer the conversation back to the more interesting subject. "So what's his name?"

"Mark," she says. "I met him at Spring Fest during sound check. He plays in that band The Nitwits."

I suck air through my teeth dramatically. "Unfortunate name."

"It is, but they have a good sound. Mark says they're considering changing it to Clancy's Revenge."

"Not the greatest name I've ever heard, but a solid improvement."

"My thoughts exactly."

"So did he ask you out or did you ask him?"

"He asked me," she says, blushing pink with the memory. "Shut Up had just finished our sound check, and he came up to me back stage and said, 'I like your sound.' Well, Marty overheard him and jumped in with something like 'Oh, I bet you think girls can't rock,' or some shit, and Venus told her to shut up, and Kate tried to break it up. And by then they forgot all about Mark, and I was left standing there apologizing for my crazy bandmates."

"Sounds about normal."

Cherie nods. "Yep. So anyway, he asked me to stay and listen to their check and then he asked if I wanted to get pizza after."

"Did you?"

"Yeah. Oh, and he's how we booked the tour. One of the bands dropped out, and they needed someone to fill in."

"That's awesome! So is that all you did on your date? Talk about the band?"

Cherie bites her lip. "No. We also made out for like an hour. He's a really good kisser, knows how to use his tongue but doesn't get all slobbery." Cherie's eyes go wide. "Shit. Is this grossing you out?"

Confused, I scrunch up my face and tilt my head. "No. Why would it?"

"Because you like girls."

I snort out an annoyed laugh. "And guys. I'm bi, Cherie. I can appreciate a good boy-girl kiss."

"But I thought that was like… a phase."

I sigh and playfully smack Cherie on the forehead. "It's not like I'm a lesbian when I'm with Jackie and straight when I'm with a guy. I can find both guys and girls attractive. And even if I didn't, you're my friend and you can always tell me about guys you like, whether I find them attractive or not."

"I forget that you swing both ways," Cherie says. "I think it's because Jackie is so… um…"

"You can say butch. She's proud of it. And she's totally gay."

"Do you, um… like that sort of thing?" Cherie fidgets and stares at a spot on the carpet; she twirls the silver ring she wears on her thumb and doesn't look up.

Truth is, I don't know what I like. I'm not sure I have a "type." I'm not even sure that's an actual thing anyway. Kate and Jackie are such polar opposites. There's not much to compare. "You know, I haven't given it much thought. I just really like Jackie."

"Yeah, but like, do you think she's hot?"

"Hell yeah."

Cherie's jaw tenses.

"What?"

Biting her lip, Cherie finally looks up. "I guess I'm confused. Or maybe I'm just a complete moron." She takes a breath like she's going to continue and then stops. Her eyes dart around the room.

I put my hand over hers to calm her. "Spit it out. I won't get mad."

"When I first met Jackie I thought she was so freaking hot. I couldn't explain it. I mean, I'm straight." She looks at me, her eyes wide and imploring. When did I get to be the sexuality expert? I'm still figuring out my own hot mess of a life.

I shrug. "If there's one thing I've learned in the past few months it's that sexuality is pretty fluid. I wouldn't worry too much if you find another girl attractive."

"But what if I'm bi?"

"What if you are? Then again, you might be straight. The only person who gets to decide your labels is you. And if you decide you don't want a label because shit's confusing right now, that's cool too. No one says you have to have everything figured out at eighteen, you know?"

Cherie doesn't look convinced. "Do you think everyone has these kinds of random attractions?"

"Maybe. I only know my experience, and I can remember being fascinated with other girls when I was like six. There was this girl named Renee in my second-grade class. I still don't know if I wanted to be her or be *with* her, but looking back I'm pretty sure she was my first crush."

"Amber Penman," Cherie mumbles. Her gaze returns to the floor, and she stares down at it, obviously deep in thought.

"Huh?"

"She was my best friend in kindergarten. I was obsessed with her. My mom said I used to kiss her and play with her hair." Cherie's eyes grow watery. "That would make so much more sense."

"Cherie?"

She looks up at me, her eyes swimming, and she says, "Tabitha, I think I'm bi."

I bite my lip to keep from laughing. It's not her revelation; it's the completely astonished look on her face. "Welcome to the club!" I throw my arms around her. Dazed, she reaches up with one arm to squeeze back.

"I'm not going to stop shaving my armpits or anything," she says.

I shove her shoulder playfully. "I still shave my armpits, you know. But if you decided not to, that would be okay with me."

"And I don't think I'm ready to date girls."

"You don't have to. In fact, this whole conversation can stay between us if you want."

She nods slowly. "Yeah, I'm not sure I should drop that bombshell on Mark just yet."

"It's probably more of a third- or fourth-date conversation."

Cherie's laughter is stilted, but at least she's stopped staring like a deer in headlights.

"I'm bi," she says again.

"You're bi."

"That was not where I thought today would end up."

"I bring all the girls out of the closet," I joke.

"Yourself included."

"Okay, so tell me about Mark."

CHAPTER 11

"So I was thinking," Jackie says. We're lying in the tall grass behind my house and she's loosely braiding my hair. I have a feeling I'm going to look ridiculous when she's finished, but her nimble fingers feel so soothing on my scalp that I don't care. "What if we went on tour with the band?"

I twist my neck to see her face, pulling her forward with me when she tries to keep her grip on my hair. "Like actually go on tour with them?"

She tugs my head gently back into place. "Sure, why not? We're already going to the first show, and we're practically their roadies anyway. It could be fun."

I try to picture it. Sleeping in Marty's mom's van, eating gas station burritos at four in the morning. Listening to Kate drone on about her latest cause. Trying to keep Venus from murdering Marty in her sleep. "Yeah, sounds like a blast," I deadpan.

"Well, it won't be glamorous or anything, but it sure beats hanging around Decker all summer."

That does add to the appeal. Mom always works a lot in the summer. People tend to be looking for new houses when school is out. And since she started dating Dan and I started going out with Jackie, we hardly see each other in the evenings. It's not as if she'd miss me.

"What would we do for money?"

Jackie shrugs. "I've got some saved up. And we could sell merch or maybe your zine."

"Zines aren't meant to be profit centers," I remind her. "It's just for fun."

"Yeah, well, even if you only charge a dollar, it might keep us fed on the road. I'm sure most of those towns have a Kinko's."

It's not a bad idea. I wonder if I can convince my mom to let me go. Jackie's eighteen and on her own, but I'm not so sure Margaret Denton will be too keen on her sixteen-year-old traipsing across the Midwest on a multi-city tour.

"I thought we were going to try to save up for college or whatever. I just started at the mall."

"We have plenty of time for that," Jackie says. "But now we have a chance to be free and do whatever we want. Don't you want to spend the summer with me?"

"The tour's only three weeks."

"You know what I mean." She ties off the braid and releases my hair. "Just think about it, okay?"

I nod, and she kisses me.

DRUNK ON AFFECTION, I WANDER into the house after Jackie leaves to find Sparky sleeping on the kitchen floor in front of his bowl. I look at the clock. It's well past his usual feeding time. I open the cabinet, and his ears perk up immediately. By the time I scoop out some kibble, he's wide awake and panting excitedly. The food disappears as quickly as it falls into the bowl. I don't think he chews some of it.

"Sorry, buddy," I say, scratching him behind his ear. "I guess I lost track of time."

As if it's responding to Sparky's boisterous crunching, my stomach growls loudly. "Guess I forgot to feed myself too."

I get a box of mac and cheese out of the pantry and fill a pot with water. When I turn the burner on, I hear the front door open.

"Sorry I'm late, but I brought pizza!" Mom sounds strange.

I switch the burner off and follow the sound of my mom's voice into the living room. She's sitting on the couch, leaned back with an arm covering her face. She has one shoe off and her purse is lying on the floor next to the coffee table. She usually puts it on the table in the entryway.

"You okay?"

She looks up, and her eyes are rimmed with red. Almost all of her eye makeup has rubbed off. "Oh, Tabitha, I wasn't sure you were home. I brought pizza." She points halfheartedly at the coffee table.

I try to ignore the tantalizing smell of melted cheese and tomato sauce wafting from the box and ask again, "Mom, what's wrong?"

"Oh, honey," she sobs and drops her head into her hands. "I feel so stupid. Dan said he wanted to see other people. I thought we were serious."

I sit next to her on the sofa and put my arm around her. "It's okay, Mom. It'll be okay." I try to rub her back, but she leans on me, and I'm thrown off balance. I don't know what to say. Moms aren't supposed to cry on their kids' shoulders, are they? Her body shakes with sobs, so I continue to stroke her back and hope she says something soon. I don't know what to say. Should I ask what happened? Why isn't there a guidebook for stuff like this?

"He was so good to me," she says between sobs. "And handsome. Didn't you think he was handsome?"

Ew. Gross. "Well, um…"

"And he had his own business, his own life, and I messed it up."

"I'm sure you didn't mess it up."

"I asked him to move in with us," Mom deadpans. "And he said he didn't want anything serious. He said he's been dating two other women."

"You did what?" I cannot believe she'd do that without talking to me. She barely knows the guy and she asked him to move in to our house? What on earth possessed her to do something like that?

"I know. It was so stupid. But I thought he felt what I felt, and it's been so long since a man paid attention to me like that, Tabitha. I guess I got a little carried away. But now, thanks to my big mouth, he's gone."

I have to remind myself that he's not actually moving in with us and my mom is upset. I make an attempt at levity.

"Did you really want to be in a relationship with a man who was dating two other women? I mean, there is such a thing as an STD. Heard of AIDS? Jeez, Mom, you might have dodged a bullet there."

She tries to laugh, but it turns into a sob. "Oh my God," she says. "I have to go get tested. Tabitha, hand me my purse. I need my address book to call Dr. Baker." She holds out a hand and wiggles her fingers.

I push her hand back into her lap. "Mom, calm down. It can wait until tomorrow." I reach behind me and grab the box of tissues from the bookshelf. "Here. Take these."

She pulls a tissue out and dries her eyes, taking the last remnants of her eyeliner with the tears. "When did you get to be so grown up?" A watery smile breaks through.

"Well, I do have my own experience with heartbreak. So I'm a pro now."

She laughs, just a little, but it's enough.

"Why don't I get some plates, and we can dig into this pizza and then we can watch one of those ridiculous old musicals you love."

"Even *Thoroughly Modern Millie*?" Through her tears, her eyes light up. It's always been one of her favorite movies.

"Yes, even that incredibly weird one."

"Hey, it's supposed to be weird. It's aware of its quirks. That's part of the beauty of it. Ignore the horrible Asian stereotypes, and we'll be fine."

I playfully pat her knee. "Whatever you say." I stand up. "Go ahead and put it in. I'll be right back."

On my way into the kitchen, I grab the phone and dial Jackie's number. Venus answers.

"Hey, Vee. Is Jack home yet?"

"Not yet. Want me to have her call you?"

"No, I'll call her later. Thanks. Hey, can you tell her that my mom had a relationship crisis, so it might be kind of late?"

"Sure," Venus says.

I promise myself that I'll talk to my mom about the tour as soon as she's over Dan. I still have a few weeks before Jackie will expect a response.

I grab some paper plates and make it back to the living room in time for the overture.

When I wake up it's dark and the TV is a blur of snow and crackling white noise. I stand up and stretch and glance at the clock. It's just after two-thirty. Too late to call Jackie. So I turn off the TV and cover Mom's lower half with a blanket. She sniffs and rolls away from me. I trudge up the stairs and flop on my bed. It smells of Jackie, and my heart lurches. I hope she doesn't think I forgot about her. I hope she got my message.

I toss and turn, debating the risk of dialing Vee's house in the middle of the night. I don't think her parents would get too mad. They tend to be pretty laid back. I pick up the handset and start to dial and then hang up. Her parents may be laid back, but I'm pretty sure Venus would kill me. It can wait.

I lay back on the pillows and think about Mom. She made it through *Thoroughly Modern Millie* okay but halfway through *An Affair to Remember*, she started sobbing again. Dan may not have been perfect, but I liked that he made Mom happy.

I've never seen my mom cry before. Even when Dad left, she held her head high and hid her emotional outbursts from me. I had started to think she didn't cry, although I knew logically she probably did. Doesn't everyone? But knowing your mom cries and having her teardrops fall on your shirt while she sobs into your shoulder are two different things.

Summers, when I was a kid, Dad used to take me to get ice cream after dinner while Mom stayed home and did the dishes. I once asked him why she didn't come with us and he said, "Your mother doesn't like ice cream." When I was twelve, I saw Mom eat an ice cream sandwich at a Fourth of July picnic. It was then that I knew my parents were human. Dad lied, and Mom ate junk food. That should have been my first clue about both of them, especially Dad. Tonight I learned that behind my mother's confident, professional façade is a scared little girl who wants to be loved. In retrospect, the clues were there all along, but I suppose everyone's blind where their parents are concerned.

I don't know how long I've been lying in the dark but I'm still awake when the blackness outside begins to lighten. I fall asleep listening to birds beginning their morning song.

THE NEXT TIME I WAKE, it's late afternoon. The light streams in my west-facing window, making a cross-hatch pattern on my floor. The sound of knocking pulls me fully out of sleep.

"You awake?"

I yawn and stretch as my mom eases open my door.

"I am. Sorry I slept so late."

She waves it off. "Don't be. I let you sleep. I know I kept you up late last night."

I scoot toward the headboard, and Mom sits beside me on the bed.

"You feeling any better?" I ask.

"I'm starting to," she says. "Thanks for indulging me. I'm sorry I was such a mess."

"Mom, you were not a mess. Breakups are hard. You have a right to be sad."

She smooths imaginary wrinkles from the front of her pants. "Well, I appreciate it anyway."

"You're welcome."

Mom stands and pulls my curtains back, letting in more light. "Jackie called earlier. I told her you were still in bed, but she wants you to call her."

Damn. "I was supposed to call her last night."

"I'm sure she'll understand, honey." Mom leans over me and tucks a strand of hair behind my ear. "Are you hungry? I can make pancakes."

"Yeah, I'll be down in a few."

The phone seems to ring forever before a breathless Jackie says, "Hello?"

"Hey, it's me."

Silence.

"Jackie?"

She clears her throat. "I'm here."

"Sorry I didn't call last night. Mom broke up with Dan and she needed some serious comforting. I fell asleep on the couch. You're not mad, are you?"

"I'm not mad."

She's trying to sound upbeat, but I can hear the lie in her voice.

"Jack, you don't have to lie to me. I know you're upset."

"I'm not upset." It's obvious she's gritting her teeth. I can picture the hard line of her mouth and the sparkle in her eyes when she gets emotional. I can't help but smile.

One of the things I admire about Jackie is her passion. I know it sounds strange, but I think it's because of Kate. The thing is, Kate's passion is self-righteous, just like her activism. She's trying to prove she's better than everyone else. But Jackie. My Jackie? She's passionate because she's trying to prove she's as good as everyone else and she's pissed as hell that the world doesn't always see it. Kate sees injustices and holds a protest. Jackie sees injustices and does something about it. Both are admirable, but Jackie's response is more real to me. So anytime we argue, I fall a little more in love.

"Well, I really did fall asleep on the couch and then when I woke up and realized how late it was, I stayed awake all night worried that you'd think I forgot to call. Did Vee give you my message?"

"Yeah."

"I promise I didn't forget about you."

"Okay."

She's still tense. I wish we were having this conversation in person so I could hold her. Instead I soften my tone, trying to make it sound as much like a hug as a voice possibly can. "You can yell at me if you want. You don't have to be tough."

"I don't want to be tough." Her voice is barely audible, as though she doesn't want to be heard. "I want to be girly and sweet."

I let her words hang in the air. My out and proud Jackie still wants to be feminine.

"You *are* girly and sweet… and tough. And I love *all* of those things about you. You can be angry. You can be sad. You can be butch or feminine. You can be whatever you want to be, and I'm still going to love you."

"You love me?"

Shit. Maybe we're not there yet. My heart races as I try to come up with a way to back out of my admission. "Jackie, I—"

"I love you too," she whispers. Her blinding smile is audible, and I'm suddenly giddy.

Neither of us says anything, but I can tell Jackie is still on the line because I can hear her breathing. It's shallow and rapid. I'm sure she's feeling the same crazy, stupid excitement I am.

"Mom's making breakfast, but I'll come over later if you want."

"Sure," she says, sounding breathless.

When I hang up, I engage in a totally undignified giggle as I lie on my bed and kick my feet excitedly. I love Jackie and she loves me. When did my life get this awesome?

CHAPTER 12

"Tabitha, could you come here please?" Teresa calls me over with a wave of her hand. She's scowling, as per usual.

Teresa is my manager at The Place and she has a way of speaking to me that's more condescending than not. Whenever she beckons, I know I'm about to get chastised.

"What's up?" I ask innocently.

"Do these shirts look okay to you?" She practically towers over me, which only adds to the intimidation factor.

I study the stack of shirts she's pointing to. They're neat but not perfect. "I guess not." I know the answer she's looking for so I offer it without hesitation, even though I had planned to fold them after my break. I figured there was no point in doing it now with the store so busy.

She smirks and crosses her arms over her ample chest. "If it's not too much trouble, do you think you could fold these properly?"

"Sure, Teresa." I try to hide my face from her view because I know my expression is anything but pleasant. I've never had a good poker face.

"And when you're finished with that, someone's bratty kid left one of the dressing rooms a wreck." She practically skips back to the register where she chats with a customer while I set about re-folding a stack of already neatly folded shirts.

I'm almost finished when I hear an all-too-familiar voice in the front of the store.

"I need to get something for this weekend. Brad's taking me to Donovan's and I need to look hotter than hot." Heather's voice carries and is echoed by Molly's shrill giggle. Trailing behind the duo, as usual, are Adina and Jen.

As Heather comes into view around an end cap, I quickly fold the last two shirts and duck into the dressing room. The room is absolutely disgusting: clothing strewn all over the floor and small bench, empty hangers on every surface and a layer of something unidentifiable and sticky streaked across the mirror from the floor to about waist high. I easily take care of the unwanted merchandise, but to clean the mirror, I'll have to get the glass cleaner from the storeroom, and that means going into the store where Heather and her minions are. I swallow heavily around a lump in my throat, and I hear Jackie's voice in my head.

"You don't deserve to be treated like a doormat," I tell my reflection in the sticky mirror. "Stand up for yourself. They're on your turf." Turf? What am I, an extra in *West Side Story*? I roll my eyes at my sticky twin and square my shoulders. I swing the dressing room door open wide and it strikes something hard.

"Ouch!"

It's Molly. Great.

"Ugh, watch it, Flabby." Molly rubs her arm while managing a sneer of disgust. "Look, Heather, it's Tabitha the Whale."

Adina laughs, followed by Jen. Then Heather appears, her arms full of clothing, and I brace myself for more teasing. Molly and Jen are still giggling and Adina's laugh has tapered to a snicker as they wait for Heather's reaction. But she just stands there, looking at me with a neutral expression that I can't figure out. "Hi, Tabitha," she says solemnly.

"Hi," I say, but I'm absolutely dumbfounded. No snide remarks? No jokes? No laughter? Just "Hi"? What the hell? Molly is as confused as I am. She's staring at Heather with her mouth agape. Jen and Adina glance back and forth between the two of us, trying to decide what their reactions should be.

Finally, I give up and squeeze past them. "I've got work to do," I say. I walk away as if they're not even there. I've got a sticky mirror to clean. Someone else can help these girls with their shopping adventures.

"Not even an apology. Can you believe that?" Molly says, her voice loud enough for Teresa to hear. As expected, her head whips around and she's back near the fitting rooms before Molly can say another word.

"Can I help you ladies?" Teresa says in her best customer service voice.

I roll my eyes and duck into the storeroom before I can get myself into any more trouble. I'm sure Molly is weaving an expert tale of how awful I am, so I'll get an earful later. But when I come back out with the glass cleaner and some paper towels, the girls are nowhere to be seen, and Teresa is back at the register. I exhale a sigh of relief and walk toward the fitting rooms.

Without looking up, Teresa says, "Your friend's in the dressing room. See if she needs anything."

My friend? Surely she can't mean Heather, or worse, Molly. I hedge my bets that it's not Jen or Adina. I hadn't even spoken to them. But I drag my feet, because no matter who is in there, I have no desire to "help" them with anything. Except maybe off the edge of a cliff.

The only clue to the occupant of the room is a pair of bare feet peeking out from below the door. "Everything working okay for you?" I call out.

A pair of jeans appears over the door. "Um, I'd like these in a size six, please," Heather says. She sounds nervous, which is weird. She's never been nervous around me—not when we were friends and not since she disowned me. I take the jeans and look for the same pair in a smaller size. I try not to think about the fact that it's Heather, but I can't help it. Why did her friends abandon her and why is she suddenly being nice to me? Well, not nice, exactly, but polite at least. She did say please, after all.

"Here you go." I toss the jeans over the dressing room door.

A few moments later, I hear the lock. The door creaks open, and Heather steps out. She looks great in the jeans and fitted blue top. I'd tried the same shirt on when it came in last week and, even in the largest size, I looked like ten pounds of sugar stuffed in a five-pound bag.

Unable to help myself, I say, "You look great. Have you lost weight?"

She smiles and nods excitedly. "About eight pounds." She turns to admire herself in the three-way mirror. "And the best part? I wasn't even trying!"

"That's great." I try to smile, but I catch my reflection in the mirror. I'm most definitely scowling.

"I think it's just happiness," she says without prompting. "I started going out with Brad Mason a couple of weeks ago and since then I've been too busy to eat."

My skin breaks out in gooseflesh, and my face feels hot. "Brad Mason?"

"Mmmhmm," Heather says, still admiring herself in the mirror. "Do you know him?"

"We had first period together."

"Isn't he such a hottie?"

"Yeah, I guess."

She turns to face me with narrowed blue eyes. Her hair trails behind her as though she's starring in a shampoo commercial. "Are you blind? He's like the hottest guy in school. Or maybe you're just jealous."

"I'm *not* jealous."

Heather raises a perfectly arched brow.

"I just don't think Brad is a very… nice guy."

She rolls her eyes. "What would you know?" she says. "He probably wouldn't give you the time of day."

I almost laugh but the smell of cinnamon tickles my nose. I sniff and it's gone, but the memory lingers: Brad's sweaty hand on my back, his demanding mouth on my pursed lips.

"Whatever," I say. "Are you taking the jeans?"

She huffs. "I guess so. Can I wear them out?"

I hold out my hand. "Sure, just give me the tags."

She plucks one tag from under her arm and another from the waistband of the jeans. "You don't have to be jealous," she says, handing me the tags. "I'm sure there's someone out there for you."

Stunned, I stare at her. Is she serious? She doesn't even know me anymore and she acts as though I need dating advice from *her*?

"Actually, I'm seeing someone," I say. "Her name is Jackie and she's so much hotter than Brad."

Let her chew on that.

She gapes at me like a fish, and, without another word, I take the tags to Teresa at the register. My steps are buoyant. Heather Davidson's hold on my life is over. I don't need her approval and I certainly don't need her friendship.

WHEN I GET HOME FROM work that afternoon, Sparky greets me at the door as usual, but Mom is nowhere to be found. Normally, this wouldn't worry me, but this morning she told me she'd be home all day and we'd go out for dinner. I'd been planning my epic Olive Garden breadsticks binge all day, and my stomach is quickly growing impatient.

"Mom!" I yell up the stairs. Sparky, uncharacteristically subdued, nudges my hand with his cold, wet nose. His ears are back, and his eyes questioning. "What's the matter, boy?" He nudges me again, and I get the impression he's trying to make me go upstairs. He follows dutifully as I climb, and, when I get to the top of the stairs, I know something's wrong. I can hear faint music over the sound of Mom's shower, which makes the pipes groan when the hot water flows. I keep telling her we need to get that fixed.

Her bedroom door is open, so I go in. We've never been much for privacy in my family, at least not between me and my mom. We've been known to have entire conversations with one of us on the toilet. The bathroom door is open a crack, and I peek my head in.

"Mom, I'm home." My voice echoes over the linoleum and bare walls.

No answer.

"Mom?" I push the door open all the way. The room is filled with steam, and the shower looks empty. As I step closer, I can see that Mom is sitting in the tub with the shower on full blast. Her arms are curled around her bent knees, and she's crying. No, not crying, sobbing. Her face is only slightly redder than the rest of her. Flushed skin from the heat of the shower and the shame of tears make her look like a completely different person. Maybe she is.

I shut off the tap.

"Mom, what happened?"

She looks up at me and shivers. I wrap her in a towel the way she used to do for me when I was small. I grab another towel and try to pull some of the moisture from her hair. I gently push her soaked bangs out of her eyes and smooth them away from her face.

"I didn't hear you come in," she says, looking at me as if she's never seen me before. Suddenly her eyes go wide. "Oh, Tabitha, I'm so sorry! We were supposed to go to dinner. Just let me get dressed and we can go."

"Shh," I soothe. "Don't worry about it. We can order a pizza or something. For now, let's get you out of that tub and into something warm."

She nods, and I can't help but notice how defeated she looks. Our roles have completely reversed: I'm now the mother and she's the child. As she stands on shaky legs, I wrap her in the towel and help her out of the slick tub. Then I get pajamas from her dresser and lay them out for her and go back in the bathroom to hang the wet towels. When I come back, Mom is dressed and sitting on the edge of the bed looking dumbstruck.

"Mom, please tell me what's wrong."

She looks at me, blinks twice and then sobs. I rush to her side and wrap my arms around her.

"I can't believe I was so wrong about him. Why do I always pick the wrong guys?"

I rub soothing circles into her back. "Who? Dan?"

She nods. "He's married with two kids. Twins." She sniffs. "And they're only eight years old!" She sobs again, and I pull her close.

Meanwhile, I process the information. Was he dating two other women, plus Mom *and* his wife? What a scuzzbucket. My mom does not deserve this. No woman does.

"It's not your fault, Mom. He's the asshole for cheating on his wife *and* his family."

"I feel so stupid, you know? I should have known."

"You couldn't know," I say. "How could you have known?"

"He's a dentist, Tabitha. I could have easily done some research on him. It's not like he doesn't have an office staff or patients."

"So you were supposed to interrogate everyone who works for him and stalk his patients? Mom, that's nuts."

"Well, it would have been better than finding out this way."

"What way?"

She laughs. It's actually more like a bitter puff of air with a single "ha" tacked on. She wipes the tears from her cheeks. "I went for a teeth cleaning."

"At his office?" I can't decide if I'm appalled or proud. On one hand, it takes some serious balls to go after what you want. But on the other, it's seriously pathetic to beg a guy to take you back. Women shouldn't grovel like that, especially not my beautiful, caring mom.

"I thought I could make him see reason. Maybe he'd see how fabulous I looked and beg me to go out with him again. I'd have another shot and I wouldn't make the same mistakes." And I'm sure my lack of poker face has come into play because she says, "I know how stupid it sounds, but I was desperate. So, I'm sitting there in the exam room, lying back on that stupid chair with a baby pink bib clipped to my new Calvin Klein dress and I see a family photo right there on the wall. At first I'm thinking, 'Okay maybe that's his sister and her kids or an ex.' So when the hygienist comes in, I ask. She says, 'Oh, that's Dr. McMahon and his wife. Aren't the twins cute?' and I say, 'He's married?' And I practically vomit on that stupid bib when she says, 'Yeah, Brenda's our office manager. She checked you in.'"

"Oh my God!"

"Then I had to sit there while that girl cleaned my teeth and try to get out of there without being seen by Dan."

"Mom, that's awful." I can't imagine what she's feeling. Embarrassment? Humiliation? Anger? Hurt? Probably all of the above. At least when Kate and I broke up, I only had my broken heart to contend with. This is another level of heartbreak altogether.

She wipes the last of the tears from her face. "I'm sorry if I scared you," she says. And suddenly she looks like my mom again, as if the confession erased the pain, or the complete vulnerability of the last few minutes is gone, and she's simply put on a brave face.

"You didn't," I say, trying to smile for her benefit.

"Good." She takes a deep breath and exhales it slowly. "I'm feeling better. Why don't we go out anyway? I'll get dressed and meet you downstairs in twenty?"

I narrow my eyes at her. Her puffy eyes have dark circles under them. She looks as though she needs a nap rather than a night out. "Are you sure?"

"I'm sure."

Reluctantly, I get up, keeping my eyes on her the whole time. She gives me a more genuine smile, and it convinces me enough that I head for my room.

"Tabitha," Mom says, and I pause with my hand on the door frame. "I'm so glad you're here, kid."

"Me too."

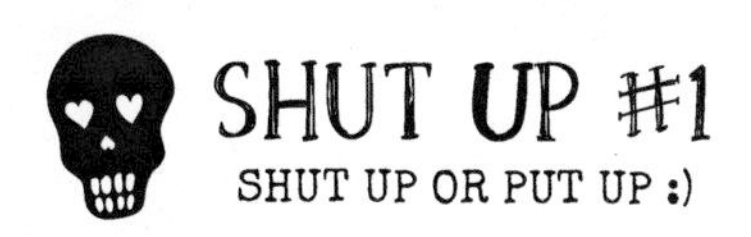

Welcome to the first ever issue of Shut Up, the official zine of the band of the same name. While we're on tour all subscribers to Rage Mart, Material Grrrl and Decked Out will receive our band's zine instead. Our loyal friends, Jackie and Tabitha, will be helping us out while we're on the road. Check out the back of the zine for our complete tour schedule, previously published in Decked Out.

NEW TOUR DATE!!!! - Don't miss it!
July 11 - LaCrosse, WI at McFly's

Shut Up is Marty DeVane (guitar), Kate Goldberg (bass), Cherie Wong (vocals) and Venus Jones (drums).

A TRIP TO THE RAGE MART
By Marty DeVane

It's okay to be angry, my fellow Riot Grrrls. We've been silent for long enough and it's time the world hears about our pain and anger and madness. It scares them, but so what? We've been scared our whole lives. Let's turn the tables and be the rage-filled monsters for once. We don't want to be seen as little girly girls. Simple vessels for you to put your emotions into in the hope of getting laid. We're sick of being reduced to wives, mothers, girlfriends. We want more. I want to rule the world with my music. I want more than romance. I want a career. I want friends. I want money. I want success. I don't want you.

I'm angry and I am going to express it. You'll just have to deal.

So tell me, what makes YOU angry?

****

It makes me angry when white girls want all women to be seen as tough. Black women are begging to be the love interest instead of the sassy sidekick or the angry black woman. Let's represent ALL women, especially women who look like me.

~Venus

CHAPTER 13

For the fourth Sunday in a row, I'm stuck closing the store with Teresa. I don't mind working on weekends, but Sundays are the worst, because it's only the two of us and we work open to close. At least today I have plans with Jackie after work. She won't tell me what, so I brought a change of clothes in case my work attire is too dressed up for our date.

I'm in the back of the store vacuuming when Jackie arrives. Teresa slams the cash register drawer closed and gives me a pointed look. She nods her head in Jackie's direction. Did I tell her Jackie and I are dating? I'm not out at work, but maybe I let it slip. Teresa is definitely indicating Jackie with all the cervical gymnastics she's doing. I nod and smile at Teresa, who looks at me as if I'm an idiot. She makes a beeline for me at the back of the store, and I turn off the vacuum.

Before I can ask what's up, she whispers, "Do me a favor, will you?"

"Okay..."

"Keep an eye on that girl," Teresa says, nodding again in Jackie's direction. "She looks… suspicious." Her lip curls on the last word as if it leaves a bad taste in her mouth.

I'm speechless. I look at Jackie and try to see what Teresa sees but all I see is Jackie's sweet smile that can light up a room. Her narrow shoulders are barely larger than a child's. She's tiny. Barely five-foot-two. When we cuddle on the couch, she curls her entire body against my side and we hardly take up my twin-sized bed. How on earth could anyone think Jackie looks "suspicious."

"That's just Jackie," I say. "We're uh… friends."

I hate lying like that, but it's not actually a lie, is it? Jackie is my best friend. *And* my girlfriend.

"Oh," Teresa says. "Sorry."

I shrug it off and flip the switch on the vacuum. Jackie browses until it's time for us to lock up.

"I'll just be a few minutes," I tell her. "Teresa needs to count the drawer, and then I'll meet you outside."

"Okay, babe," she says softly. "I'm parked by the Sears entrance."

When she's gone, Teresa pulls the gate over the entrance, and I fold the remaining disheveled shirts. I finish all my closing tasks early, so I go to the register.

"Want some help?" I offer.

"Sure," Teresa says. "Can you double-check the deposit for me?"

I start counting. Teresa watches me intently, and that makes me stumble and have to start over, but eventually I get it counted. "Two sixty-seven, eighty-seven. Same as you."

"Cool," she says. "Let's seal it up."

I pull the adhesive strip on the envelope and seal it tightly.

"Teresa, why did you tell me to watch Jackie earlier?"

She shrugs and busies herself with organizing the pen cup. "We've had a lot of shrinkage lately."

"Right, but why Jackie?"

"I'm sorry?"

"Well, you didn't tell me to watch that mom and her two kids who came in right before her."

"She was pregnant," Teresa says. "I doubt she was going to steal anything."

"Remember last week when I found those empty hangers in the dressing room? That was a mom. We never did find that red shirt."

Teresa clears her throat. "You really shouldn't tell people that we're in here counting money," she says.

"You didn't answer my question."

"I just thought she looked suspicious, okay? I'm sorry if I offended you. Can we drop it?"

I bite my lip. Jackie wouldn't drop it, but Teresa's my manager. I can't stand up to her if I want to keep my job. Can I?

JACKIE'S LEANING ON HER CAR with her arms crossed over her chest. It's sexy. I try my best sultry walk toward her, but I get the feeling I look like I've got a limp. I decide it's best to walk normally, and when I get to her I throw my arms around her. She nuzzles my neck but then pulls away before it can get too heated. Girls hugging won't raise eyebrows, but girls making out in the mall parking lot? I'm not so sure we could get away with that.

"So what's this big plan?" I ask.

"It's a surprise." Her smile stretches from dimple to dimple.

"I guess I can handle that." I walk around to the passenger seat and look over the top of the car at her. "Not even a hint?"

"Nope, no hints. That will ruin the surprise. Now will you get in before mall security gets suspicious?"

Her words are reminiscent of what Teresa had said, but I don't mention it. I'm too excited about my surprise and don't want to ruin it by bringing up something that might make Jackie upset.

She backs out of the parking space. We take a left out of the mall entrance and I wrack my brain for all the places that are south of the mall.

"Donovan's! Is it Donovan's?"

"Nope."

"I hope there's at least some food. I'm starving." I glance sideways at her, but her expression gives nothing away. "Am I dressed okay? I have a change of clothes in my bag if—"

"You're not going to trick me into giving it away," she says. "So just sit back and enjoy the ride."

I can't sit still, though. So I turn on the radio and try to find something that will distract me until we reach our destination. I hit all of her presets and the tape she has in the player, but nothing seems right. "Mind if I switch this out?"

"Go ahead," Jackie says, making another left.

I lean forward to get a better view out the windshield. "Okay, now I'm really lost. There's nothing out here."

Jackie laughs. "Just relax, will you? There's some more tapes in the console." Without taking her eyes from the road, she flips it open with a flick of her wrist. "Take your pick."

After a thoughtful search, I settle on an old standby: The Slits.

"I think Shut Up's new song sounds a lot like this," Jackie says, turning up the volume. "Listen to the chorus and bridge."

I close my eyes and let the music wash over me. It does sound familiar, but different at the same time. Like something from a dream.

"You know, I never thought I'd say this, but Shut Up's is better." Jackie shakes her head as though she can't believe what she's saying.

"Right? I mean, it needs work, but it's definitely got better lyrics. And that chord change right before the chorus? Way better."

I look up as we're turning down a road with a sign labeled, "Historic Binn Cannery."

"Look, I'm not trying to rain on your parade here, Jacks, but an old factory where they give tours to bored grade schoolers? Doesn't seem like good date material." We took a field trip here once when I was in third grade. It was really dull, so Heather and I ended up making daisy chains from the wildflowers growing around the structure while a white-haired man prattled on about Prohibition Era businesses. It's eerie today, though. No one else is here. "I think they're closed."

Jackie sighs, but it's not from frustration; her smirk makes it seem more like amusement. "Will you just go with it?"

I lean back in my seat. "Fine."

"Vee's aunt, you know that white chick Donna who married her Uncle Marvin?"

"Yeah?"

"She's on the historic preservation board and she helped me set this up."

I'm still dubious about the quality of a date at the cannery, but if Jackie went out of her way to make it special, I'll go along with it. For now.

Jackie pulls her car up alongside the cannery's main building and motions for me to get out. She pops the trunk and pulls out a blanket and a picnic basket. "Can you grab that cooler?" she says, and I notice the tiny Igloo on the back seat. My stomach grumbles at the thought of food, so I'm definitely committed to seeing this through. I haven't eaten since breakfast.

"Follow me," she says.

We wind our way through the tall grass and wildflowers to the opposite side of the building where a large flat area has been mowed in a lopsided rectangle. Jackie spreads out the blanket and motions for me to sit. She methodically unpacks the picnic basket and arranges our meal. She hands me a paper plate and gestures for me to help myself. She's brought what can only be described as a feast. Two kinds of salad, garlic bread, linguine with a rich garlic-butter sauce… and more bread. She's even packed some kind of fancy, flavored sparkling water and plastic champagne flutes. And for dessert, Venus's mom's famous red velvet cake, with extra frosting. She's thought of everything. I want to savor it slowly, but my stomach protests loudly and I dig in with fervor.

By the time we're finished eating, the sun is sinking below the tree line and fireflies emerge in sporadic flashes of fluorescent green. I lie on my back and wait for the stars to come out while Jackie puts everything back in the basket. Then she lies beside me and pulls me close.

"This was a great surprise," I say. "Much better than Donovan's."

I hear, rather than see, her smile. "Oh, I'm not done yet."

I tilt my head in time to see a mischievous grin fade from her lips. "There's more?"

"I'll be right back," Jackie says, pulling away and rising to her feet.

I prop myself up on my elbows to see where she's going, but she's disappeared into the tall grass. She's gone long enough that I'm starting to worry, when a bright light illuminates the side of the factory. I look around for the source of the light and see a small, round ball of light in the distance behind me. It flickers like a projector, so I turn back to the building and the opening to a movie plays on the makeshift screen.

Just then, Jackie reemerges from the grass with a gigantic smile on her face. "Surprised?"

"How did you do this?"

"I've got connections," she says.

I can't decide whether to look at Jackie or the screen but when I hear the actors begin to speak, I finally pull my eyes from my gorgeous girlfriend and focus on the movie. Jackie wraps her slender arm around my shoulders and kisses my cheek. It only takes me a minute or two to figure out it's *Ladies and Gentlemen, the Fabulous Stains*. I've been wanting to see it since someone wouldn't stop talking about it at a Riot Grrrl meeting.

"How did you get this?" The movie was never in theaters; the girl who brought it up only had a vague memory of it from late-night cable.

Jackie lowers her gaze and rubs the back of her neck. "I just asked around. Cherie's cousin had a copy she taped off TV."

"Thank you," I say softly and without tearing my gaze from the screen. "This was the best surprise."

"I love to see you smile," she says and snuggles close to my side.

I hadn't realized I was smiling, but now I definitely notice. My smile grows wider. This is the best night.

When Jackie drops me off at home, my mom's car isn't in the driveway. I check my watch. Still early. Mom probably won't be home for another hour.

"You want to come in?"

Jackie kills the engine. We race each other up to my bedroom and throw our jackets to the floor. Her lips are on mine before I can get the light on.

"I wanted to kiss you all night, but I didn't want to interrupt the movie," she says. "You look so sexy in this." She runs her hands up my thighs under the fabric of my babydoll dress, lifting it a bit higher. Her hand rests on my butt and she squeezes it firmly, which makes me giggle.

"What about you in these jeans?" I say to her. "I mean, have you seen yourself?" I take her hand and twirl her playfully. In return, I get a thousand-watt smile. We sway back and forth, dancing to the rhythm of our heartbeats instead of music. Jackie tucks her head under my chin and rests her cheek on my chest.

"I like when you make me feel small, like a girl."

I scrunch my neck up to try to see her face. "Um, I don't know if you're aware of this or not, but you *are* a girl."

She swats at my arm gently. "No, I mean you make me feel feminine, like I'm Meg Ryan in one of those cheesy romantic comedies your mom's always watching."

"Are we talking *Sleepless in Seattle* Meg or *Joe Versus the Volcano* Meg? Ooh, or maybe *When Harry Met Sally* Meg?"

"Doesn't matter. All of the above."

"You're right. You're way hotter than Meg Ryan."

Jackie stops dancing and fixes me with her dark eyes. "No, I mean… it's nice to be the love interest. To be the one who gets the happy ending." She sighs wistfully. "Maybe it sounds stupid, but I never thought I'd have that. Hell, I never even thought I'd have a girlfriend."

"I would have said my odds were pretty low, too."

There's a flicker of displeasure on her face, a hint of subtle tension in her brow, but it's gone so suddenly I may have imagined it. Just in case, I pull her close and resume our silent dance. She relaxes into my arms and hums an unfamiliar tune as her hand drifts higher on my thigh.

DESPITE OUR PICNIC FEAST, I wake up the next morning positively ravenous. I think it's because we ate so early. By the time Jackie left around one—after a heated make-out session—I crashed. So by eight o'clock, my stomach is protesting loudly and I'm in the kitchen digging through the pantry for an errant Pop-Tart or cereal bar. I've decided today is the day I talk to Mom about going on tour with Shut Up. Mom's mostly over Dan, and, after last night, I've decided I'd rather spend a few weeks with Jackie than folding shirts with Teresa. I will need to put in my notice, though. I could join them for the last two weeks of the tour.

My search of the kitchen isn't yielding much in the way of a quick breakfast. Mom hasn't gone shopping in weeks. I start writing a list. Maybe she's planning to go this afternoon.

I jot down a few items before resuming my search for anything resembling food.

Finally, I find a bag of chocolate-covered pretzels on the top shelf behind an unopened bag of flour. It's evidently the last thing in the house that doesn't need to be cooked. It's not much of a breakfast, but it will have to do.

The squeak of the sliding glass door catches my attention, and I turn to find my mom sneaking in from the backyard with her shoes in her hand. She tries to close the door more quietly than she opened it, but it squeaks again and she grimaces. "Shit!" she whispers.

"Don't worry about it. I'm up."

Mom nearly jumps out of her skin as her shoes go clattering to the floor. Her right hand flies to her chest. "Tabitha, you scared me."

I take in her rumpled appearance. Her blouse is half untucked, her skirt drapes crookedly over her hips and her usually perfect hair is a matted mess in the back.

Even though I'm about ninety-nine percent sure I know the answer, I ask, "Did you even come home last night?"

Mom blushes a blotchy shade of pink, and she bends to pick up her shoes. "I should have called, honey. I'm sorry."

"Is everything okay?" She looks so lost. Maybe she had another run-in with Dan or his wife.

She brushes her hair out of her face and tries to smooth it down. "Um, yes. I fell asleep at a friend's house."

The way she says the word friend makes me think she's leaving out crucial details, but I don't press her. I'm just glad she didn't come home to find Jackie and me half-naked in bed or she'd never let me go on that trip. I clear my throat. "Well, um… I'm going to find something for breakfast. I have to be at work at nine."

Mom smiles awkwardly and shifts on her feet. "Right. I should uh, probably get a shower and change." She crosses the room and gives me a kiss on the cheek on her way upstairs.

I try not to think about what my mom might have been doing last night or with whom as I munch on my breakfast of chocolate-covered pretzels and coffee. Maybe I'll ask her about the tour tomorrow when she's in a better mood.

CHAPTER 14

"Have you asked your mom about going on tour yet?"

Jackie and I are sitting in the fenced area of the park watching Sparky chase his tail and enjoying the first warm summer day of the year. I close my eyes and tilt my head back into the sun. Not too hot yet. It warms my face and I can almost feel the vitamin D jolt in real time. "Not yet," I say.

Jackie sighs. "You promised."

I tilt my head down and open my eyes. I haven't filled her in on Mom's relationship drama. Not fully anyway. "I will, Jack, but things are really complicated right now. Mom had a full-on meltdown the other night. I found her crying in the shower! And she's coming home at weird times." I pause and wait for a reaction. I expect Jackie to be shocked or something. Anything but the unsympathetic eye roll I get.

"You mom is a grown woman. She can handle herself." Jackie's brown eyes are piercing; her lips are set in a firm line. It's hard to disagree with her. I don't want to argue.

"I know that, but…" I can't finish the sentence because I know Jackie won't understand. She's so fiercely independent, but I'm not. I'm just not. And anyway, I'm all my mom has.

After Dad left we promised that we'd look out for one another no matter what. I can't leave her now when she needs me the most.

Jackie looks at me expectantly. "Just give me a little time," I say. I have no clue how I'm going to broach the subject with my mom, but I'll figure something out. I hope. "What's the rush, anyway?"

"The tour starts in a couple weeks, Tabitha. Time is running out."

"But we still have *weeks*," I insist. "Why are you pushing this? Can't we enjoy the fact that I have a Saturday off for once?" I gesture at the park and the warm sunlit grass all around us. Sparky dashes to my side and sits expectantly waiting for me to throw whatever he must have assumed I had in my hand.

"Go away, dumb dog." I show him my empty hands, and he sulks over to Jackie. She scratches him under his chin. This pleases him, I guess, because he bounds off to resume chasing his tail.

Jackie picks at the grass and tosses the torn blades in the air. They flutter and land far less dramatically than I think she intended.

I still her hands with my own. "Jack, what's wrong?"

She doesn't look up. "Nothing." She shoves my hands away and picks at the grass again, this time more violently.

"You're not a very good liar," I say.

Jackie scoffs. "Yeah, well…"

I let her sit and stew, knowing she'll eventually tell me what's bothering her. I can't be sure, but I sense that it's more than the tour.

Finally, I get my answer.

"Vee's parents want me to get a job." She shreds a blade of grass and picks another.

I furrow my brow. "Well, that sounds reasonable."

"I have to get a job and start paying them rent or move out." She rips the fresh blade in two and then tears it again and again until it's in tiny pieces.

"Ah."

Jackie stands up, brushing the tormented grass from her lap. "God, it's just like my parents all over again!"

"Come on, it's not. You know that." I say these words gently, but I don't think Jackie takes it that way.

"What do you know? Your mom is so freaking accepting of you, but my mom? Yeah, she basically told me I'm going to hell." She throws her arms up in frustration. I can see the pain of not having her family accept her has finally caught up to her. She talks a big game, but I know Jackie. She hurts just as much as the rest of us. The difference is Jackie doesn't like to show it.

"You're not going to hell." I stand and put my arm around her.

She tries to avoid eye contact and blinks away some unshed tears. "I feel like I'm already in hell sometimes, you know?"

I'm not sure I know what she means. Does she mean Decker? Us? Living with Venus? I'm too scared to ask for clarification. Maybe there's more to her wanting to go on this tour than I thought.

"Is this why you want to go with the band so badly?"

She nods. "I don't want to be left behind when Venus leaves. I figure I can buy some time with her parents if I get out of their hair for a few weeks."

"That makes sense."

"And I really want you to go with me," she says, circling my waist with her arms. "I want us to go together. I don't want to be apart from you at all this summer."

My heart picks up tempo at the familiar swoop in my belly. "I don't either."

She presses her face to mine. The tips of our noses touch and she looks like she only has one eye. I bite my lip to keep from laughing.

"Then go with me," she says.

I close my eyes and take a deep breath. "I'll try," I say. It's all I can promise, and I hope it's enough.

THE REC CENTER IS NEARLY empty the following Tuesday when I arrive for the Riot Grrrl meeting, and I'm ten minutes late. Cherie and Kate sit in chairs facing each other playing cat's cradle with an old shoelace. Marty sits nearby with her notebook; her pen flies across the page. Standing along the far wall are two girls from Central High whose names I can't remember. And Venus is sitting on the floor, using one of the chairs for a makeshift drum.

"Where is everyone?" I ask.

"It's summer," Kate says. "They're probably doing other stuff."

I nod. It makes sense. "Where's Jackie?" I ask. Trying to avoid eye contact with Kate, I direct my question to the group. This is going to get awkward pretty quickly if Jackie's not here.

"I thought she was with you," Venus says between beats. She doesn't look up.

"She said she was riding with you."

Venus shakes her head and keeps drumming. "She told me she was covered. I assumed that meant you two were coming together."

"Maybe I should go find her," I say to myself.

"I'm sure she's fine," Cherie says. Her smile is reassuring. "Why don't you come sit with us?"

Kate's eyes dart in my direction but she doesn't say anything. I take the seat closest to Cherie and tuck my feet under me. "I haven't played cat's cradle since middle school." Heather and I used to play all the time but we'd eventually get caught in a looped pattern of the same three setups. Cherie and Kate seem to have a method to keep it from being too repetitive. Or maybe it only seems that way.

"My fingers hurt," Cherie says. "And I have to pee." She lets the shoelace drop and Kate catches it. "You want to play?" Cherie stands and gestures for me to take her seat.

I catch Kate's expression, expecting her to look as shocked as I am, but instead she smiles and threads the shoelace across her wrists and then her fingers.

"Come on," she says. "You know you want to."

Something in her eyes looks like a dare, and it's almost like the first time she kissed me. My stomach flutters, and I have to clear my throat to conceal my nerves.

"Okay." I switch seats. Cherie bounces off to the bathroom, leaving me and Kate staring at each other.

Kate tilts her chin to indicate I should begin, so I pinch the two X's made by the thread with my thumb and forefinger. Then I pull it out and under, transferring the game to my hands. We go back and forth a few times in silence. It's nice not being uncomfortable around Kate. And if I'm being honest with myself, I'd like to be her friend again.

"Your hair looks good like that," I say.

"Thanks," she says, moving the cradle to her hands. "It's gonna be a bitch to grow out, so I may be stuck with it for a while."

"You'll make it work." I pinch the thread between my fingers and loop it back on itself, but I slip and it pulls tight on my wrist. "Shit."

Kate giggles at my clumsiness. "We had a good streak going, too. Here, let me help you." She takes my hand and unwinds the shoelace.

Her hand lingers a second too long and I pull away. Blushing, I rub my wrist.

"Sorry," Kate mutters.

"It's okay."

"No, I mean about… us."

"Oh."

"Yeah. Oh." Kate tucks her hair behind her ear. "I know I look like I have my shit together, but I'm honestly just trying to figure stuff out like everyone else."

I want to say something. I *should* say something. But I'm in shock. Did Kate actually apologize to me? Did she apologize to me *and* admit she's floundering like the rest of us? I have no idea what to do with this information.

"You don't have to say anything," Kate says and, for a moment, I wonder if she can read my mind. "I wanted to say I'm sorry and I did. I'd like to be friends if you're amenable."

Something about Kate using her five-dollar words thaws the icy shards in my veins that are left over from when she shattered my heart.

"I think I'd like that," I say.

"You would?" Kate's eyebrows nearly reach her hairline.

"What? You thought I'd spit in your face?"

"You know, the thought had occurred to me." There's a tremor in her voice that supports her words. The fact that Kate was worried I'd reject her makes me want to laugh. I place my hand over hers.

"It's in the past." It's not a full redemption, but it's all I've got.

She smiles at me, and I think everything might be fine between us.

"What the hell is this?"

Jackie stands in the doorway to the rec center, one hand still on the door. She's backlit so I can't quite see her face, but I can tell from her posture she's angry. I pull my hand back from Kate's.

"Jacks, I was wondering where—" I smile, but Jackie cuts me off before I can finish.

"I should have known. I was always the second choice, wasn't I?"

"Jackie, it's not like that."

I stand and take a few steps forward. Now that I can see her face, I can tell that lurking below her anger is a layer of hurt. Tears sparkle in the corners of her eyes, but they refuse to fall. I reach for her, but she jerks her arm away.

"Don't touch me!"

"Kate and I were just talking," I say, pleading with my eyes for her to believe me. "She was apologizing for what happened between us."

Jackie's hands are clenched into fists at her sides. If I didn't know her so well, I might think she was gearing up for a fight, but she's trying to control her breathing. I want to hug her, but I'm afraid she might take off if I step any closer. Her eyes dart from me to Kate as if she's trying to decide if we're telling the truth. Out of the corner of my eye I can see that all the other girls are now staring at us. Waiting, I hold my breath.

"Then why were you holding hands?" Jackie's voice is calm. Too calm.

"We were playing cat's cradle," I say with a laugh. Immediately I regret it.

Jackie's gaze drops to the floor, and she blinks back tears. My stomach lurches with guilt. I'd rather she yell at me than this. I can't stand to see her in pain.

"Why are you lying to me?" she asks quietly.

Kate stands up and steps between us. "Jackie, you got this all wrong."

I grab Kate's arm. "Don't."

Jackie's eyes lock on my hand where it rests on Kate's bicep. Her jaw tenses as a single tear falls. She turns on her heel and is out the door before I can catch up to her.

"Let her go," Kate says. "She'll calm down and then you can reason with her."

"Kate, look, I said I'd try and be friends, but right now you need to mind your own fucking business."

Kate's blue eyes grow wide, and she clamps her mouth shut. I take off after Jackie.

I FIND JACKIE AT OUR park, sitting on our usual bench. She doesn't look up when I approach and folds in on herself when I sit down beside her. Her arms crossed tightly across her chest, she stares straight ahead.

"Jackie, please talk to me."

"I have nothing to say," she says, calmly.

"Well, I do. Please let me explain."

She stares, unblinking, at the horizon. I take her silence as a complicit go-ahead.

"Kate and Cherie were playing cat's cradle and when Cherie went to the bathroom, I picked it up. That's all. Kate apologized for the way she treated me and asked if we could be friends. The string got tangled on my wrist and Kate was helping me get it off. That's all that happened."

Jackie swallows and nods. Her voice is barely audible. "You two looked pretty cozy when I came in."

"Well, I can't speak for Kate, but I was just killing time while waiting for you. Honestly. Nothing happened. And nothing's going to happen. That's history. Promise. I love you."

I wait for a response, but she keeps staring off into the distance. I reach for her hand, and she doesn't pull away. After a few moments, her shoulders relax, and her eyes shift to the ground in front of our feet. And then slowly, she curls her fingers around mine.

"Here. I got you this," she says, reaching into her pocket with her free hand. She holds up a tiny red box with a silver bow around it.

I stare at the box, then glance at Jackie. "How? When?"

"It's why I was late." She lifts it higher. "Take it."

Tentatively, I reach forward. What if she still rejects me? What if I've broken things beyond repair? But then logic creeps in amid my anxious thoughts. She wouldn't give me a gift if she was breaking up with me. Just open the damn box.

Slowly, with my hands shaking, I lift the lid. Sitting inside the box on a bed of black tissue paper is a key on a heart-shaped keychain. I hold it up and look to Jackie for clarification.

"It's to my car." She shrugs. "I thought it would help if you had your own key for when we go on our road trip with the band."

"I haven't talked to my mom yet," I confess.

"I know," she says, leaning her elbows on her knees and hanging her head. "I thought it might be an incentive."

I can't help the smile that spreads across my face. "It's definitely an incentive."

She looks up, her brown eyes shining. "So go with me."

I set the key back in the box and replace the lid. I watch the way the fading sunlight plays on the glittery surface of the box. "I don't know if I can."

"You haven't even asked yet!"

"Well, no. But it's also because I don't know if I want to go. I really need the money from my job, and Mom's still a mess."

Looking defeated, Jackie asks, "So is that a no?"

"No," I say. I hold my hand out and she takes it, albeit reluctantly. "It's an 'I don't know.'"

She pulls her hand away. "You're just so fucking indecisive, Tabitha!"

I narrow my eyes. There's something more to what she's saying than simply the trip. "What's that supposed to mean? Indecisive about what?"

"Never mind," she mumbles.

I stand on shaky legs. "No, tell me what you mean or I'm leaving."

She shakes her head.

"Tell me."

She glances up at me and then folds her arms across her chest. I brace myself for whatever it is she's about to say. It's still not enough.

"Me and Kate," she says, as if that explains everything.

"I told you that was nothing. I'm not indecisive. I chose you."

"No, I mean.... Okay, you *say* you're bisexual,"

"And?" I challenge.

"You've only dated *two* people." She pauses and fixes me with her gaze. "Both girls."

"So?"

"So, that makes you a lesbian, my friend. A big, fat dyke with a big ole dyke girlfriend." She gestures wildly with her hands while she talks, but I can't move my feet.

Just leave, I tell myself. *Walk away.* But I can't; I'm frozen. Except for the tears that stream down my cheeks and tickle my neck, I'm still. Jackie's eyes blaze with the release of saying something that's been weighing on her mind. Her breathing is rapid and barely audible over the blood pounding in my ears. She raises her eyebrows, waiting for me to speak, but like my legs, my lips are immobile.

"Nothing to say? Or are you still deciding?"

That breaks me. My tears come hotter and faster as fury burns through me.

"Fuck you," I manage on an exhale. "Just fuck you."

Finally, I find my ability to walk and I leave her there on the park bench. I drop the key on the sidewalk.

I WANDER BACK INTO THE rec center. I'm not ready to go home. These days Mom has been extra chatty, and I don't want to explain my fight with Jackie. I push through the doors. As the artificially cooled air hits my skin, the heat from outside condenses and makes me feel sticky all over. I yank my hair into a messy ponytail and tie it in a knot at the base of my neck.

A few more girls have showed up, including Monique. I take a seat next to Cherie.

"What'd I miss?"

"Monique is moving to Detroit, and Venus wants us to recruit more black girls so she and Jackie aren't the only ones in our Riot Grrrl group."

"Why should we have to seek out people based on race?" Kate says. "If they don't want to join, we can't make them."

"Yeah, I'm all for including more diversity," Marty adds, "but we can't force it."

Monique rolls her eyes. "See, this is what I'm talking about!"

The room erupts in a cacophony of arguments with Marty shouting to be heard over it all. But I'm so numb it barely registers. My mind is swimming, and tears sting my eyes.

"You okay?" Cherie says. She's the only one not caught up in the argument. "Where's Jackie?"

I shrug. "I don't want to talk about it."

"I get it," Cherie says. "But I think Jackie might want to." She points at the door where Jackie stands with the red box in her hands. Her face is calm; her posture is contrite. I walk across the room toward her.

"I was just leaving," I say as I try to push past her.

She grabs my arm, but it's gentle. "I'm so sorry, Tabitha. Can we go outside and talk?"

I follow Jackie out back to the picnic table where she consoled me after Kate and I broke up. This time we sit side by side, but we don't touch. I cross my arms over my chest and wait for her to speak.

Jackie takes a deep breath. "I didn't mean it," she says. "I knew as soon as it was out of my mouth that I was wrong. But when I get angry, I just can't help myself."

"You hurt me," I say. "I need you to be okay with my sexuality or this won't work."

"I know," she says, wiping a tear from my cheek. "And I am."

"Then why did you say it?"

Jackie closes her eyes and sighs. Then she turns to face me. "Because I know you, and I know what will hurt you the most. I'm not proud of it, but I've always done it. I go for the jugular because if I can strike first, the other person can't hurt me as bad." She smooths her hand over my hair. "But this time it didn't work."

"It didn't?"

"No, it didn't. It didn't work because you left my present on the sidewalk. And I realized something."

"What?"

"That we have the power to hurt each other very, very deeply. And we have to be careful with each other or we'll break our own hearts."

I bite my lip, but it's no use. A tear hits my cheek and then another and another. Sniffing, I wipe them away. "I'm sorry," I say. "I won't be friends with Kate if you don't want me to."

"I can't ask you that."

"Yes, you can." I take her hands in mine. "I love you, Jack. I'd do anything for you."

She smiles. "I love you, too."

When I kiss her, the world falls away, and I feel whole again.

CHUBBY BUNNY NO. 2
by Tabitha Denton

Bisexuality is not a phase.

Bisexuality is not a phase. Bisexuality is not a phase. Bisexuality is not a phase. Bisexuality is not a phase. Bisexuality is not a phase. Bisexuality is not a phase. Bisexuality is not a phase. Bisexuality is not a phase. Bisexuality is not a phase. Bisexuality is not a phase. Bisexuality is not a phase. Bisexuality is not a phase. Bisexuality is not a phase. Bisexuality is not a phase. Bisexuality is not a phase. Bisexuality is not a phase. Bisexuality is not a phase.

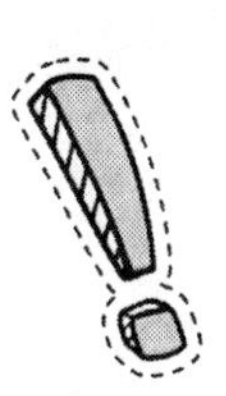

IT'S NOT A PHASE!!!!

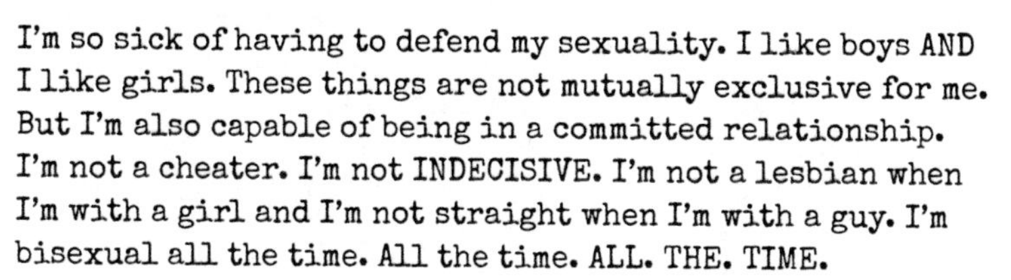

I'm so sick of having to defend my sexuality. I like boys AND I like girls. These things are not mutually exclusive for me. But I'm also capable of being in a committed relationship. I'm not a cheater. I'm not INDECISIVE. I'm not a lesbian when I'm with a girl and I'm not straight when I'm with a guy. I'm bisexual all the time. All the time. ALL. THE. TIME.

LAW OF ATTRACTION

I guess opposites are supposed to attract or whatever, but that doesn't apply to me. At least not when it comes to gender. If I find someone attractive, gender is irrelevant.

The first time I realized a person's gender didn't matter to me? It was a Saturday afternoon and k.d. lang was on MTV. The video for "Constant Craving"—an evocative black-and-white fever dream created by a short-haired sex bomb in a partially unbuttoned striped shirt—played boldly against a sea of sameness on my TV.

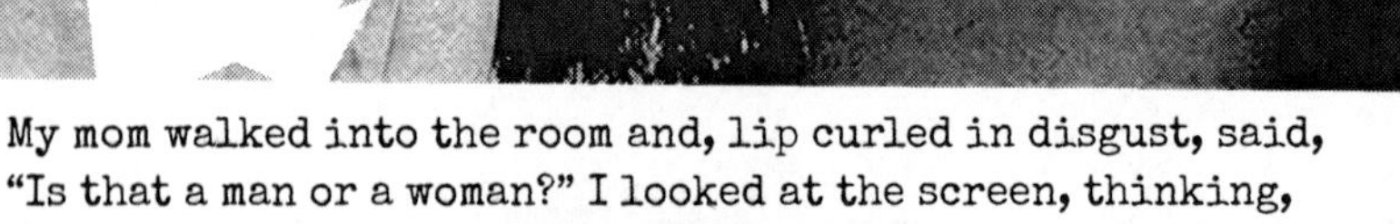

My mom walked into the room and, lip curled in disgust, said, "Is that a man or a woman?" I looked at the screen, thinking, "Does it matter? That person is gorgeous."

Maybe I should have realized then that I was bisexual, but it took me a couple more years to figure it out. My celebrity crushes are a litany of androgyny and gender ambiguity. David Bowie, Boy George, Prince, Annie Lennox, and the list goes on. The line between male and female had blurred and I was obsessed. I cut my hair short (which turned out not to be a good look for me) and dressed in the most boyish clothes I had. Sadly, my gigantic boobs got in the way of my dream of androgynous glory, but I still found myself seeking out anyone who could straddle that line effortlessly.

CHAPTER 15

Shut Up is leaving on tour in less than a week, and the girls' nerves seem to be frayed raw.

"You're missing your cue!" Marty yells. "Again!"

"Sorry," Cherie replies. "But Venus keeps going faster."

"I'm just following Kate's lead," Venus says.

"You're the fucking drummer!" Kate shouts. "We're supposed to follow you."

"Jesus Christ! This is getting us nowhere." Marty slips her guitar over her shoulder and storms off the stage.

"Girl, get back here. We need to run through the new song!" Venus's voice carries, but Marty ignores it and pushes through the double doors. In the growing darkness, the cherry from a cigarette flares to life.

"I'll go talk to her," I offer. "I think you guys are just stressed about the tour. Maybe she'll listen to an outside voice."

"I'll join you," Jackie says. She tosses an unreadable look over her shoulder that causes Venus to nod.

"What was that about?" I whisper.

Jackie waves it off. "Nothing. Let's go talk to Marty."

I watch her intently, but her expression is neutral. I shrug it off and push open the doors. Marty is standing outside the entrance with her arms crossed. The butt of her cigarette is already stubbed out on the ground. She sees me and lights another.

"Those things are so bad for you," I say, as if I hadn't smoked to get in with Mike.

"If you came out here to lecture me, no thanks," Marty says, taking a long drag. "I just needed a break and I'd like to enjoy it in peace."

"We didn't come out here to lecture you," I say. "Right, Jackie?"

She shakes her head.

"We just thought maybe you'd like to vent to someone not in the band—an outsider, if you will."

Marty scoffs. "Right."

Jackie tilts her head and narrows her eyes. "Don't attack us. We're just trying to help."

"Yeah, I'm sure. You'll probably run and tell Venus everything I say."

"Marty, that's not fair," I say.

"Oh, so you chicks aren't tight? Ain't she your girl?"

I feel Jackie's body tense at the obvious mocking tone Marty is employing. She steps into Marty's personal space. "Yeah, she's my girl. What of it?"

Marty laughs. It's bitter and dangerous. "Oh, so now you're going to get all ghetto on me?"

"Marty, stop!" I glare at her, but she ignores me.

"Oh, fuck this," Jackie says. "You talk to this crazy bitch on your own, Tabitha. I'm going inside to talk with 'my girl' before I do something I'll regret."

Jackie pulls the door open with more force than is necessary, but I'm glad she's got our back to us because Marty chooses that moment to roll her eyes.

"Marty, ease up. You're going to get your ass kicked if you don't stop talking like that."

"So it's okay for her to call me 'white girl' but if I mention them sounding all ghetto, *I'm* wrong?" She throws her hands in the air and ashes rain down on us. "I'm so sick of this politically correct bullshit!"

I'm not sure what to say to that. I think it might go beyond being politically correct, but I don't want to egg Marty on. She's already worked up. She stubs out her second cigarette and lights another.

"Can I have one of those?" I ask. I haven't had a cigarette since my days hanging with Mike behind the 7-Eleven, but right now I need something to do with my hands. Marty lights it for me and I inhale. I cough and sputter as the piercing burn of the smoke hits the back of my throat. "God, I forgot how disgusting this is."

Marty laughs, and this time it's warm and friendly.

"I'm sorry I offended Jackie," Marty says after a bit.

"Thanks, but maybe you should tell *her* that."

Marty nods slowly. "Yeah." She takes a drag of her cigarette and blows the smoke over our heads where it floats for a second before dissipating. "I feel like no matter what I say, Jackie and Venus are going to jump all over me for it."

"Maybe, but you have to try. And maybe listen once in a while." I stub out my cigarette and dust off my hands. "You ready to go back in?"

She lifts her hand with the cigarette between her index and middle fingers. "I think I'm going to finish this first."

"Okay. Maybe… try to be a little less confrontational, okay? Jackie and Venus are your friends."

Marty raises an eyebrow as though she doesn't believe me, but then she smiles. "Yeah, okay. Thanks, Tabitha."

Mom lets me borrow her car for the show in Aurora so that Jackie can leave immediately after with the band. Well, she doesn't exactly *know* it's for the concert or a date with Jackie. I told her I needed to borrow the car, and she didn't ask. Jackie's car is in the shop, so she's not taking it on tour. It's weird to be the one driving with Jackie riding shotgun, but it's the good kind of weird. She massages the back of my neck with her left hand and sings along with the radio.

"Your voice is beautiful," I say. "You should form your own band."

Jackie shrugs. "Maybe. I don't really like being onstage."

"Neither does Cherie. But she says it's different with a band. She doesn't feel so on display."

"That boyfriend of hers seems pretty cool," Jackie says. The change in subject is her way of telling me the topic of her singing in a band is dead.

"Yeah, I think it might have something to do with being raised by two moms. He's pretty progressive for a guy in a punk band."

And since he convinced his bandmates to give Shut Up a spot on their tour, the Riot Grrrls have collectively decided we like him.

Jackie nods and then turns to stare out the window. She doesn't say anything else until we pull up outside The Pit. The marquee boasts the names of the bands: The Nitwits, Donkey Kart & Shut Up.

"Well, the girls easily have the best band name of the three," I say.

"Mm-hmm."

I kill the engine and turn toward the passenger seat. "Jackie, you've been awfully quiet tonight. Are you okay?"

She shrugs, her preferred method of communication tonight. "I guess so. I wish you were going on tour with us, that's all."

I close my eyes and take a deep breath. I'd chickened out about asking my mom. I don't know why, but I couldn't find the courage to ask. Or maybe I'm worried she'll say no and then I'll feel even worse. Or maybe she'd say yes. I'm not sure I'm ready for Jackie to know what my morning breath smells like. Would she expect things? We've done lots of stuff from the waist up, but the idea of being totally naked and having orgasms together, I don't think I'm ready for that. Not yet.

"I know," Jackie says when I don't respond. Her voice sounds heavy, and my heart twinges. "Let's just enjoy the show, okay?" She smiles at me, but it's forced. It's better than no smile, I guess. At least she wants to be happy.

I open my door and step out into the sweltering July night. "I'm glad this venue has air conditioning." Apparently some of the later dates are in venues with barely any circulation, let alone cool air pumped in. I think I'd die.

"Come on," Jackie says, wrapping her arm around my waist. "Let's get you inside before you melt."

CHERIE DOES HER USUAL SPIEL calling the girls down to the front, and the crush of bodies closes in on us. It's hot and sweaty, but I don't care. Jackie squeezes my hand, and we share a smile just as Shut Up rips into their first song.

My friends are cool. They're in a band and they are legitimately, undeniably cool. And not in an abstract, I-like-this-music kind of way. But in an own-the-stage, make-you-want-to-start-your-own-band kind of way.

Dancing comes easier this time. I raise my hands over my head and thrash with the crowd, not caring what I look like or who's watching. This is my territory… and theirs. In this moment, girls own this place and that's powerful. For the first time in my life, I'm part of something bigger than myself. It may not solve world hunger, but it matters. Just like Kate's obsessive need to protest, and Marty's passion for Riot Grrrl, and Cherie's unapologetic femininity, everything has its place. Even "Flabby Tabby" dancing at a concert is part of it.

I look around to take it all in. Jackie and I are once again front and center, but this time we are surrounded by dozens of girls who came to see Shut Up play. I recognize a few of them, but most are just here because they heard about a punk girl band and want to be a part of the moment. I can't believe it. I'm part of something, and it's not dorky or cheesy. It's real. I'm real.

Over the roar of the band and crowd, Jackie's voice meets my ears. She's singing along and dancing wildly. Joy radiates from her like heat from the sun. She's part of it, too. Without asking, I know she's experiencing the same feeling. Now, more than ever, I love her. I still can't believe she wants to be with me, but I know it's true. And more importantly, I believe it. I feel it deep in my bones.

When it comes down to it, I don't want to say goodbye. "Don't go." I lean my forehead against Jackie's.

"I've got to go on tour. I promised Vee."

"What about me?" I choke back tears and try not to pay attention to the band waiting impatiently behind us.

"You'll be fine," Jackie says, stroking my cheek.

Marty rolls her eyes. "Seems kind of shitty to me that you'd leave your girlfriend all alone to follow us around on tour."

"See?" Venus says. "That's exactly what I'm talking about. Nobody asked your opinion. But you gotta offer it up. Like we all supposed to listen to your ass just because you talking."

Both Marty and Jackie turn to face her. Marty looks terrified; Jackie is grinning. Marty swallows hard and opens her mouth, but Venus cuts her off.

"No. I'm done with your bullshit, girl. You say racist shit all the time and you talk over everyone and bark orders at me like I don't have a brain of my own. This is why I want Jackie on tour with us. I need backup when you start all your white-girl craziness."

"But—"

"Uh-uh." Venus holds up her index finger in front of Marty's face. "Unless it's specifically related to the band or a life-and-death situation, you don't speak for the next twenty-four hours."

Marty looks to Cherie and Kate for support. But they pretend to find the ground very interesting.

"This is for your own good, Marty. So I don't kill you."

Jackie hides her laughter behind her hand, and I have to bite my tongue to keep from saying something stupid. I'm not entirely sure what this blow-up is all about, but I have a feeling it's been brewing for some time. Jackie's hand rests comfortably on the small of my back and she leads me away to Mom's sedan.

"That was weird," I say when we're a comfortable distance away.

Jackie furrows her brow. "What?"

"Venus blowing up like that on Marty. That came out of nowhere."

"Oh," Jackie says. "Yeah, it wasn't really out of nowhere. Venus has been holding back for a while."

"Why does she hate Marty so much?"

"She doesn't. It's just… Look, I know Marty is your friend and all, but she says some really problematic shit sometimes. It's racist and ignorant, and with Monique back in Detroit and you occupying my time, Vee's been dealing with most of it herself. She's tired."

"Don't you think you're a little hard on Marty, though?"

Jackie takes a step back. "Actually, I don't think we're tough enough!"

"Oh, come on. She's not racist. She's just…"

Jackie places her hands on her hips. A challenge. "Just what? Tell me what she is, Tabitha."

"She's white," I say. "Like me."

"Maybe that's the problem."

"What are you saying?"

"We're… different. That's all. Venus and I deal with a lot of shit living in Decker that you probably don't even notice."

"You think I don't see it? Shit, the other day when you came to pick me up for our date, my manager thought you were shoplifting just because of what you look like. I know what you're up against."

"It's not the same as living it, though, is it?" Jackie looks sad and defeated. I've disappointed her somehow and I don't know how it happened. I reach for her hand, but she doesn't twine her fingers with mine the way she usually does.

"Jackie, I'm trying," I say. "Please don't shut me out."

"I know, but we keep coming up against issues. And I think maybe those things are differences in the way we see the world. Maybe it's good that we're taking a break from each other."

A break? I don't want a break. I want Jackie. But I don't want her to see the disappointment in my face, so I focus on the space between our feet, and what I say is, "Sure."

SHUT UP #2

Tour diary Day 0

Hey, party people! Well, it's here: the Shut Up Semi-Midwestern American Tour. We can't wait to see you at one of our shows. Don't forget it's girls to the front, as usual, and we won't stop rocking until the venues kick us out, so bring your ass-kicking/dancing shoes. Oh, and feel free to bring your fellas to the show. Just remind them that our set is all about the ladies and they'll have to take a back seat.

Speaking of back seats, if you see a girl struggling with a guy in a car, don't be afraid to interrupt the potential amorous happenings to protect a fellow grrrl in need. If it's consensual, you'll only have egg on your face, but if it's rape, you'll be helping someone from a humiliatingly terrifying ordeal.

And don't forget to look out for each other at parties and concerts and whatnot. We've got to stick up for each other. We saw this girl the other night getting catcalled by some asshole and we got up in his face. You'd be surprised how quick these assholes back down when they find out we're willing to stand up for ourselves. Just be careful. Only do this in large numbers. One or two girls will not seem threatening to a trucker or a frat boy.

Also, it's not a bad idea to keep a rape whistle or some mace on you. It's not your fault if you get assaulted but man, it ain't gonna hurt to be prepared.

Thanks, and we'll see you at the show!

Tour diary Day 1

Well, our first show in Aurora rocked. The fans at The Pit were great. A lot of them came out to see The Nitwits and Donkey Kart, but I think it's safe to say we converted them. We sold all of the tapes we allotted for the show and had to dig into our stash for later gigs. We'll try to have more in time for the shows late in the tour, but just in case, I'd plan on getting there early if you want one.

We're also working on some new songs that we hope to have ready for our La Crosse show. So if you're planning on coming out for that one, you'll get to hear some brand-new stuff. That's all for now.

Shut Up!

CHAPTER 16

I SLEEP IN AFTER THE concert. I have the day off from work, and the only thing I have planned is roadside trash pickup duty. But that's not until later in the afternoon. I snuggle into my pillows and catch the barest hint of Jackie's scent. I miss her already, and she's only about an hour away in Rockford. This is going to be a long three weeks.

I finally drag myself out of bed around noon and shuffle downstairs in a fog. As much as I love sleeping in, I almost always regret it. It always seems like a good idea until I spend the first two hours after I wake up in a complete and total stupor.

"Morning! Or should I say afternoon?" Mom smiles and hums to herself while she cleans the kitchen counters. Yesterday's dishes are soaking in the sink.

"Hrngh." I drag myself to the pantry and pull out a box of cereal. I think it's Cap'n Crunch. To be honest, I don't care as long as it's food. I grab a bowl and some milk and plant myself at the kitchen table. Mom's still humming. How can she be so chipper?

"I heard you come in last night. You were out kind of late. Where were you?"

"With Jackie," I say around a mouth full of what is *definitely* not Cap'n Crunch. I think it might be Corn Pops, though. I take another bite.

"You're with her a lot these days." It sounds more like a question than a statement and it's loaded and ready to fire. My defenses are immediately up.

"Well, she is my girlfriend."

"Tabitha." Mom stares at me as if she's looking for a different answer. "Don't be silly."

I drop the spoon into the bowl and it splashes milk on the table. "What's that supposed to mean?"

"Aren't you just about done with this…" She pauses and lowers her voice to a whisper as if anyone could hear her from our kitchen. "Lesbian phase."

I'm not hungry anymore. I pick up my bowl, plunk it down in the dishwater with a satisfying splat. I turn to face her with my hands on my hips. "It's not a phase, Mom. And I'm not a lesbian; I'm bisexual. That's not going to change."

Her face lights up. "Well, that's great then! You can choose a nice young man to date. What about that Bernbaum boy? Didn't you used to run around with him?"

I roll my eyes at her and try my best to stay calm. "Mom, it doesn't work that way. Besides, Mike and I aren't even friends anymore."

Mom frowns and goes back to cleaning the countertop.

"I thought you were okay with this," I say. "You said Kate and I were cute together."

"You *are* cute together. I don't understand why you have to date this Jackie person."

I take a deep breath. "Because I love her, Mom."

Mom waves me off. "You're sixteen. You have no idea what love is."

"You got married at eighteen. Jackie's eighteen."

"That's different, Tabitha. It was a different time. And you can't marry Jackie."

Her words hit me in the center of my chest, and I'm shocked to find I'm still standing. Certainly a blow that hard would have thrown me across the room.

Finally I find my words. "Maybe I can't marry Jackie, but I'd rather be on tour with her and the band right now than standing in this room with you!"

I turn on my heel and practically run back to my bedroom and slam the door. I haven't done that since I was twelve. It feels good.

WHEN I COME DOWNSTAIRS LATER, Mom's car is gone and the kitchen is clean. There's a note on the counter:

Tabitha,

I had to show a house, but I'll be home for dinner tonight. We can talk then.

Love, Mom

I crumple it into a tiny ball and leave it for her to find. I'm still angry and I want her to know it.

WITH MARTY, CHERIE, VENUS AND Jackie on tour, it's my job to handle Riot Grrrl's weekly assigned stretch of road cleanup that's part of our agreement for use of the rec center. I recruited two other girls to help so we won't have to spend all day in the hot sun, but only Bennett has shown up. She only started coming to our meetings a couple weeks ago, and I think she's trying to score points, but I don't care. At least she showed up.

Fifteen-year-old Bennett is a short, pale, round-faced girl with jet black hair and golden-hazel eyes who seems to have an obsession with Hello Kitty. Everything she wears has the tiny Japanese cat depicted on it. But that's the sum total of what I know about her.

She steps out of her mom's station wagon wearing yet another Hello Kitty shirt and skips over to me. I'm already wearing my county-sanctioned safety vest and I hand the other one to Bennett.

"I wish this came in pink," she says with a frown.

"Yeah, they're not very stylish."

"Or flattering." Bennett drapes the neon orange vest over her shoulders. It won't close around her belly but it nearly hits her knees.

My vest is the larger size, but there's no way I'm giving it up. She'll have to deal.

"So normally we split up, but since it's just the two of us, I think it's best if we stick together. Grab a trash bag and some gloves, and we'll get started."

"Do I get a stabby stick?" Bennett asks, making a jabbing motion with her empty hand.

"Over by the tree," I say. "With the trash bags." I toss the third vest onto the grass near our stuff and head west. Bennett catches up to me and stabs at the small amount of trash we find. Every time she spears something, she giggles.

I'm so not in the mood for this.

"I don't think my mom believed me when I said I was picking up trash," Bennett says after a few moments of silence. "She wasn't going to bring me, but I convinced her at the last minute. Joke's on her, though, because you were here and now here we are picking up trash."

"Here we are," I mutter.

"How come you aren't on tour with the band? I thought you were friends with all those girls. You're always together."

"I um… I have to work."

Bennett nods. "Makes sense. I'm sure touring with a band that's just starting out wouldn't be very lucrative. It's not like they're Nirvana or anything."

I stab a faded Fritos bag and then an empty paper cup. I drop them in my trash bag.

Bennett keeps chatting.

"Of course I don't know if I'd let my girlfriend go out on the road with so many pretty girls. Not that I'm gay or anything. I have a boyfriend. But I'm just saying."

I'm trying to hide my frustration with Bennett, but a sigh escapes.

"Not that I think Jackie would cheat on you or anything. I'm just saying it would make me nervous."

"I'm not worried."

"That's good," Bennett says. She presses her lips together into a taut smile. "I bet they don't even sleep in real beds on tour, right?"

I nod. Her words barely register amid the sounds of cars passing. I try to block it all out and focus on my feet. One step at a time.

"There's not much trash," Bennett says. "I thought there'd be more."

"We still have to do the other side," I tell her. "We'll cross up there by the sign." I gesture with my stick at a sign that says "40 miles to Rockford" and I wonder what Jackie is doing. They're probably in the middle of sound check right now.

I can't believe I yelled at my mom. She'll never let me go on tour now. The pressing sting of tears burns my eyes, and I blink to clear them.

"You okay, Tabitha?" Bennett asks.

I sniff. "Yeah. The sun's bothering my eyes is all. I should have brought sunglasses."

"We'll have to remember that for next time," she says, smiling. She's a sweet girl, even if she does talk too much.

I smile back at her and clear my throat. "So, tell me about this boyfriend of yours. What's his name?"

Bennett giggles and bounces on the balls of her feet. "His name is Geoffrey, but spelled with a G."

"Sounds like a classy guy," I say, trying not to laugh.

"Oh, he is," she gushes.

I let Bennett ramble on about Geoffrey and try not to think about Jackie or my fight with my mom. It doesn't work.

CHAPTER 17

I FEEL SO LOST WITHOUT Cherie, Marty and Venus… even Kate. I didn't realize how quickly I became attached to the sisterhood of being a Riot Grrrl. Our meetings have fizzled; it's usually only me and a couple other girls on any given Tuesday. Bennett does most of the talking, and I sit in silence. I miss the days when we'd run out of chairs because we were stuffed into Marty's basement. The rec center seems too big. Or maybe I feel too small.

I am completely untethered without Jackie. It only takes a few days before I start noticing, really noticing, how monochromatic Decker is. It's not only the racial whiteness, although I notice that too, but it's as if I'm living in grayscale. The finer details are missing. There is a serious lack of contrast, and now so is my only link to something bigger and better than this—Jackie.

On my way home from work, I buy a tub of Manic Panic. I figure if I'm craving color and life, why not create some of my own. An hour later, my hair is purple, and I've cut myself some blunt, baby bangs. It's not the greatest haircut ever, but it's not half bad for self-styling. I turn and admire my new punk hair in the mirror. "Well, it's an improvement," I say to my reflection.

The bathroom, however, isn't looking so good. Along with some pretty heinous stains on the tiled countertop, purple-splotched towels litter the bathroom floor. Mom is going to kill me if I don't get this cleaned up.

WHEN I'M THROWING THE TOWELS—AND a ton of bleach—in the washing machine, the phone rings. I have to run to catch it before the machine picks up, so I pick up the handset in the kitchen. The cordless is still upstairs in my room.

"Hello?"

"Hey!" My hands shake when I realize it's Jackie.

"Hey, yourself," I say. "I miss you."

"I miss you too." She sounds wistful. Maybe our break is over.

"So what's going on?" I'm still breathless from my run from the laundry room, or maybe it's the surprise. She sounds older, wiser—or maybe that's just me romanticizing things. I miss her so damn much. Hearing Jackie's voice after a few days apart makes my chest burn with anxiety. I want to see her so badly. I bite my lip as I try to hold back tears.

"Well, the band is off doing sound check for tonight's show, so I thought I'd call. How are things in the hotbed of activity known as Decker?"

"Dull as hell," I say. I twist the phone cord around my fingers and hop up on the kitchen counter. My breath is starting to even out, and the tears have been contained for now. So I try to have a normal conversation with Jackie. "I um, dyed my hair."

"Really?" She sounds excited. "How'd it come out?"

"Purple," I say. "Very, very purple." I hold my breath. She's always saying how much she likes my hair. Maybe she wouldn't want me to change it.

"I bet it looks hot." Now I know I'm not imagining things. She's flirting again.

I let out a shaky breath. I hadn't realized until that moment that I was worried she'd called to break up with me. "Well, you'll have to see for yourself."

Jackie sighs. It's wistful and a little sad. "Wish you were here, babe."

"Me too." I kick my legs against the lower cabinets. "But the tour will be over before we know it, and then you'll be back here and you won't be able to get rid of me."

Silence. Did we get disconnected?

"Jacks, are you there?"

"I'm here," she says. Her voice is low and it's lost the ebullient tone of moments before. My heart beats faster.

"Is something wrong?" I hold my breath and wait for her response.

"I'm not sure I'm coming back to Decker."

My stomach drops to my feet, and my heart flutters wildly. Is this what a panic attack feels like?

"What do you mean? You have to come back."

"I won't have any place to live," she says.

"But what about Venus's house? You can get a job, and they'll let you stay if you pay rent."

"They're moving," she says. "Now that Vee has graduated, they're buying a condo in Florida."

"But Venus… the band!" I can't get out more than a word or two at a time. Forget forming sentences. Jackie may not be coming back to Decker. How can this be happening?

"Vee starts college in the fall. The band knows. We were talking about it on the way to Milwaukee."

Tears splash my cheeks, and I don't even try to stop them. "Where will you go?" I ask.

"I've got family in Chicago still. A cousin I could hit up for a place to crash. I'll figure it out."

"Jackie, you can't leave me here."

"You can come with me."

"I've still got two years of high school left. And I doubt my mom would let me pack up and move in with my girlfriend. She's accepting, but that's a stretch even for her."

"Yeah." Jackie sniffs. Is she crying too?

Silence stretches between us. How will I survive my junior year if Jackie isn't here with me? There has to be something we can do.

"Jackie, have you thought about calling your parents?"

"No, Tabitha. No way. I'm *not* doing that. I can't do that."

"But—"

"I said no. Now drop it."

"I just want you to come home."

"I know."

She's quiet again. And then, "So tell me more about this sexy new look of yours."

Through the tears, I manage to laugh. As I explain my new style, I resolve to figure out a way to get Jackie back in Decker for good, no matter what it takes.

If Jackie isn't coming home, I'll have to go to her.

When I walk into work the next day, Teresa's jaw drops. She pulls in a sharp breath through her teeth. She points at me and then crooks her finger for me to follow her. Teresa leads me to the back room and closes the door behind us.

"Tabitha, what did you do to your hair?" she asks.

Ignoring the ridiculousness of her question I reply, "I colored it. Do you like it?" I turn around and mess it up to get more volume.

"It doesn't matter what I like," she says. "The Place's employee handbook says no unnatural hair colors. You're going to have to change it back." She crosses her arms over her chest and waits for me to speak.

"I don't want to change it back. I like it."

Teresa purses her lips and exhales loudly through her nose. "Well, then I'm afraid I'm going to have to let you go." She holds out her hand. "Name tag, please."

"What?" I think she's joking. I almost laugh, but she glares at me. She's serious. When I don't comply, she raises her eyebrows and taps her foot. She's still holding out her hand. "Teresa, come on. No one cares what color my hair is!"

"Obviously they do or it wouldn't be in the handbook, which you agreed to, by the way. You signed an agreement when you accepted this job and you're in violation. If you're not going to change your hair back to a natural shade, then you can't work here. It's as simple as that."

I unpin my name tag from my shirt and drop it in her open palm.

"I'm really sorry about this, Tabitha," she says. "Call me if you change your mind."

"I won't," I say. I shove the door to the store open and let it slam behind me. "I hated working here anyway!" My voice carries through the store, and a woman near the fitting rooms stares at me open-mouthed. "What are you looking at?"

She lowers her eyes and pretends to be interested in the skirt she's holding.

Teresa's voice behind me is cool but threatening. "Please leave before I call security," she says.

"Whatever." I stomp out of the store and walk all the way home instead of taking the bus.

I GO TO BED EARLY and I'm still there when Mom leaves for work in the morning.

She calls out from the hallway, "Everything okay, Tabitha? I thought you were working today." She pushes my door open.

"I'm not feeling very well, Mom. I think I'm going to hang out here today."

"Are you running a fever?" She places a hand on my forehead. "You're not warm."

"It's just a headache," I lie. "I'll be fine. I just need some rest."

"Are you sure? I could cancel my morning."

"I'm fine. Really."

"Okay," she says reluctantly. "But call me if you need anything."

When she's gone, the house grows overwhelmingly silent. I need to get out.

I take Sparky for a walk, but my heart's not in it. Jackie should be here. I let the dog off his leash at the park and sit on our bench. It's too hot to be outside, but I don't care. The burn of the sun is better than the torture of being home with my thoughts.

No girlfriend and fired from my job. I'm *such* a winner.

When Mom comes home, I'm back in bed, but she thinks I've been there all day.

"You'll feel better if you get out of bed. Come on downstairs, and I'll make something for dinner."

I raise an eyebrow. My mom is actually a pretty good cook, but lately we've been ordering out. When we're both home, that is.

"Don't look at me like that," she says. "I still remember how to cook. Now get your lazy butt out of that bed." She swats at my foot. I laugh and snuggle deeper into my covers.

It's the smell emanating from our kitchen that finally pulls me from the comfort of my bed. Something garlicky and sweet is sizzling away on the stove, and there's something in the oven.

"Smells good," I say, leaning on the counter. "Need any help?"

"How about you set the table," she says.

Because it's only the two of us, it only takes me a couple of minutes to grab plates and utensils, so I sit in a kitchen chair and watch her work. The dark circles that had taken up residence under Mom's eyes have faded, and she's looking more like her old self. I wish there was a way to screw Dan over the way he did Mom.

"How's your headache?" Mom says as she tosses a pinch of salt in one of the pans. "Did you take something for it?"

"I'm feeling better." I don't elaborate.

"Where are your friends? I haven't seen Jackie or Cherie around much lately. And you haven't mentioned Kate or Marty in weeks."

She seems to have forgotten our argument about Jackie, so I don't mention it.

"They're on tour," I say. "Their band got asked to open for Cherie's boyfriend's band. I thought I told you."

Mom shrugs. "Maybe you did. I've been kind of out of it lately."

"Jackie went with them."

Mom pauses but doesn't look up. "I see."

I pop a carrot in my mouth from the salad bowl. "I miss her like crazy." I hold my breath and wait for Mom's reaction.

"Maybe it will be good for you girls to have a break from each other."

I let my breath out in a huff. "That's what Jackie said."

A smile tugs at the corner of Mom's mouth. "Smart girl."

"Why don't you like her?"

She drops the spoon in the pan and turns to face me. "Tabitha, I never said I don't like her. I worry about you. A lot has changed for you this year, and I'm your mother. It's my job to make sure you're healthy and happy."

"I am." I lock eyes with her. It's as if we both understand the challenge there. Whoever blinks first, loses.

I raise my eyebrows, and Mom turns back to the stove. "All right. I'm sorry I overreacted. I just don't want you to get hurt."

"I might," I say, thinking of what Jackie said about us having the power to hurt each other deeply. "But that's what love is, right? You give your heart to someone and trust that they'll handle it with care. I trust Jackie."

"I trusted Dan," she says. "And I think you'd agree, I put my trust in the wrong person."

"Well, you have to trust that *I* didn't."

I see her breath catch, and her lip quivers. I picture her sitting in the tub, crying, and I know where her fears are coming from. I step around the counter and rest my head on her shoulder. She strokes my hair.

"I'm trying, kid." She wraps an arm around my shoulders and holds me while she stirs. "Now why don't you tell me the real reason you stayed home from work today."

CHUBBY BUNNY NO. 3
I'm Not a Specimen

I don't think we talk nearly enough about how much it sucks to be a teenage girl. Not only do you have all the normal teenage problems, but you're also female, which affects how everyone sees and treats you.

I'm also walking around with my girlfriend on my arm. (Not a girl who's a friend but a GIRLfriend.) So we get rude comments and stares and glares and we also get catcalled and whistled at. None of that is cool, man. None of it. But it happens. And I'm sure it happens to a lot of you too.

I also get called fat, ugly, a bitch. Why can't I just BE?

Why do I need a label?

Meanwhile I label myself: bisexual, female, Riot Grrrl, punk, Tabitha.

I need these labels. They are mine.

But I refuse to be labeled by men. I refuse to be labeled by society and I REFUSE to be labeled by anyone but me.

I'm SPENT a poem by Tabitha Denton

I spend my spare time folding shirts at the mall;
I'd rather be making out with my girlfriend.

I spend the money I make folding shirts on new CDs;
I'd rather be moshing in the pit to a grrrl band.

I spend years trying to be invisible;
I'd rather be someone else.

I spend years running from myself;
I'd rather be somewhere else.

I spend hours daydreaming about my girlfriend;
I'd rather be hers than invisible.

I spend too much time fighting;
I'd like to be me.

CHAPTER 18

Once Mom knows why I'm sitting around the house, she works pretty hard to make sure I don't spend the rest of my summer in bed eating. She leaves me a list of chores that fills an entire sheet of notebook paper. It was our trade-off for letting me go to the last of Shut Up's shows in Chicago.

I haven't told Jackie yet because I want it to be a surprise, and I'd like to get through at least half the list to make sure it's doable. The first thing on the list is cleaning out the garage. We have a stack of boxes that dates back to before I was born. Holiday decorations and family heirlooms are mixed in with clothes that no longer fit or are no longer in style. It takes me the better part of the day to get through it all, but when I do I have a hefty load for donation and several bags of trash at the street. The remaining stuff has been sorted and labeled for my mom to store. The only thing I keep for myself is a picture of me and Dad. I look about six years old and I'm sitting on his knee. He's smiling at the camera, but I'm grinning up in adoration at my daddy. I don't remember it being taken but I remember that feeling. Why do the people I love always have to leave?

"Hey, stranger."

I look up, half-expecting it to be my dad, but it's Mike. He's dyed his hair too, only his is electric blue, and instead of dangling a cigarette from his mouth, he's chewing gum. "Nice hair," I say, unable to think of anything else.

"You too," he says. "Purple's a good color for you."

I nod, and he kicks at a crack in the driveway.

"Why are you here, Mike?"

When he looks up, his eyes sparkle with tears. "I wanted to say I'm sorry."

"Okay?"

"I have a confession," he says, flipping his blue hair out of his eyes. "I've been reading your zine."

I raise my eyebrows. I've only got a few subscribers, and Mike isn't one of them.

"I get it through an exchange," he says. "I didn't want you to know."

I don't know whether to be offended or impressed. It's not as if my zine is a secret. "I don't mind that you're reading it."

He licks his lips. "Good to know. I uh, really liked the part about not wanting other people to label you, and I realized I'd kind of been doing that. I expected you to stay the same person you were when we started hanging out and I didn't see how much you'd changed."

"That's okay," I say.

"It's not. I think I may have been blinded by my crush." He scratches his cheek, and bites his lip.

It's the first time he's admitted to it, and I'm taken aback. "I had a crush on you, too, you know?"

His eyes widen. "No, I didn't know. That's… Wow."

"It was short-lived, but believe me, I know all about being blinded by crushes."

Mike nods and lowers his gaze. He's kicking at the crack again. "Well, I guess I should go." He turns to leave, but I realize I don't want him to.

"Wait!" I call out. "Why don't you come in for a bit. I have some new music you might like."

He furrows his brow as if he's contemplating it. "Won't your girlfriend mind?"

"No, and anyway, she's out of town with the band."

"Oh yeah, I heard about the tour. Sounds pretty cool."

"Well, except for the 'all my friends are out of town' part, it is."

"Not *all* your friends," Mike says with a grin.

"You're right." I smile. It's nice to be friends with Mike again. He follows me into the house and upstairs to my room.

"I like your room," he says.

"Thanks. I forgot you've never been inside." We've only hung out at concerts, record stores and behind the 7-Eleven. The few times he picked me up from the house, he honked, and I ran out. "There's not much to it, but it's home." I put a CD in my stereo and motion for Mike to sit.

"Smells better than the parking lot of the 7-Eleven, that's for sure," he says with a laugh.

"Very true." I sit beside him on the bed, and he moves away from me. I opt to ignore it. If he's still a little on edge, I won't push it.

We don't talk for a bit in favor of listening to the music, but when the CD ends, he lies back on the bed and asks, "So how come you're not following Shut Up on tour with your girlfriend?"

I open my mouth to tell him about Mom's breakdown and my job at the mall and all the other reasons I had for staying in Decker, when it occurs to me none of those reasons exist anymore.

"To be honest," I say, "I have no idea."

Mike toes off his shoes and pulls a pack of gum from his pocket. He pulls out a piece and offers it to me, but I shake my head. So he unwraps it and adds it to the piece he's already chewing. Maybe he's quit smoking. Before I can ask, he tosses out a question of his own. "Where are they now?"

I grab Shut Up's zine with the tour dates in it and look at today's date. "Peoria."

"That's not far," he says. "Why don't you go?"

I roll my eyes at him. "How am I going to get there? Mom won't let me borrow her car. She needs it for work."

"There is a thing called the bus, you know."

"But we made a deal. I'd do some chores around the house, and she'd let me go to the last show in Chicago. I can't renege on that."

"Why not? You said yourself you don't have any reason to stay here. If you take the bus you don't need the car, and she can still go to work."

"What if she says no?"

"Who said you have to ask?"

THAT SAME AFTERNOON, MIKE DRIVES me to the bus station and buys me a one-way ticket to Peoria. It's only a few hours away, so

I should get there just as the band is finishing their set. I've shoved all the money I made from my job at The Place, minus my final paycheck, into my backpack. I plan to be back in a little over a week, so I don't bring much else. I left a note for my mom on the counter, telling her I'll be home late. I'll call her from the road and tell her the truth. A note telling her I've run off to be with Jackie would probably ensure a complete and total meltdown.

"You sure you won't come with me?" I ask him for the third time since we left my house. He thinks I'm afraid of traveling alone, but it's more like wanting someone to witness it. As if it's not real unless someone else can attest to the order of events. I want to feel real and whole, tethered to the earth again. Of course, that's why I'm going to Jackie, so maybe I'll be fine without Mike.

"Nah, this is a trip I think you need to make on your own," Mike says. When he grins, his dimples peek out from his cheeks.

I surge forward and wrap my arms around him. "I'm sorry I was a shit friend."

He pats me on the back with one hand, leaving his other dangling at his side. I think I might have caught him off guard. "We both made mistakes." The sound is muffled by my shoulder. He pulls back and brings his hand to my cheek. "You're really something, Tabitha. Jackie's lucky to have you."

His eyes say all the words he's left unsaid. A small part of me wishes I could return his feelings, that I could offer more than a vague, fleeting crush, but I know it wouldn't work. I'm in love with Jackie. I give him a gentle peck on the cheek. "I'll call you when I get back," I say. "Maybe we can hang out or something."

He nods. "Maybe I can finally meet Jackie."

"I'd like that."

THE BUS IS QUIET AND empty, and it smells like old cheese, but I choose to treat it like an adventure because it's taking me to Jackie. I owe her an apology for not going with her in the first place. I figure showing up to surprise her is the second-best option to time travel.

I pull my Discman out of my backpack and push play. As the suburbs fade into farmland, I drift into a dreamless sleep.

I MUST SENSE THE BUS has stopped, because I wake up and we're parked on the side of the road. I crane my neck to look out the windshield and see bumper-to-bumper cars, all stopped and waiting for the same thing we are. I pull my headphones off and lean into the aisle. The closest person to me is sound asleep, so I trek to the front of the bus.

"Excuse me, why are we stopped?" I ask the driver. He's reading a newspaper and eating a ham sandwich. We must have been here for a while.

"Accident," he says.

"Will it take long? I'm kind of in a hurry." I check my watch. If we don't get moving soon I could miss the show. I'm not sure where the venue is, and cabs could be scarce if it gets too late.

"Don't know," the driver says, taking another bite of his sandwich. "If someone died it could be hours."

"Hours?" Great.

"I know. It sucks," he says. "It's my kid's birthday. We got him a bike."

I don't care what he got his kid for his birthday. I want to get moving, but I nod and smile anyway. As much as I want to rail at this guy, I know it's not his fault.

On my way back to my seat, I notice that the other passengers have settled in for the long haul. A woman in the back is stretched out across an entire row, and the family who is sitting a few rows behind me is playing a card game. The man across from me is still asleep and snoring softly.

With nothing to do but wait, I take out my notebook and start writing.

By the time we roll in to Peoria it's nearly two in the morning. I've missed the show and I'm a stinky, grimy mess. At the bus station, I apply a new layer of deodorant and brush my teeth, but I desperately want a shower. Jackie told me the bands always pack up and leave immediately after the show, so I know they're either at a motel or on the road to the next gig. There's a bus headed to Champaign in the morning, so I have nothing to do now but wait.

It's only me and one other person in the waiting room, plus a security guard. There's a bank of pay phones in the back of the waiting room. I check my watch. It's officially past an acceptable time for me to be home "late." I have to call Mom.

I dial our number and wait as I hear the mechanical voice ask my mom if she'll accept the charges. I chew on my fingernails and hope she's not too pissed. The call is barely connected when she barrages me with questions.

"Tabitha! Is everything okay? Are you all right? Where are you?"

"I'm fine, Mom. Calm down."

"Do you know what time it is? I almost called the cops! Wait… you called me collect. Where the hell are you?"

I take a deep breath and lean against the wall. "Peoria."

The other stranded passenger—an older man with sallow skin and sunken eyes—watches me. Something about him makes my pulse race, so I turn my back to him. I hope he loses interest fast.

There's silence from the other end. All I hear is Mom's breathing, heavy and forced. She's furious.

"Mom?"

"Why the *hell*—?"

"I know what you're going to say, but I couldn't wait until next week. I have to see Jackie now."

"Tabitha, you're sixteen. You can't just take off whenever you feel like it."

"I was going to Chicago at the end of the tour anyway. What's the difference?"

"The difference is you didn't ask me." Her voice is measured and smooth. The calm before the raging storm. I immediately feel myself growing defensive.

"Would you have said yes if I had?" I realize how immature I sound, but the words are out before I can stop them.

I wonder if she heard me. Finally she says, "Tabitha, I want you to be happy. We could have talked about it and figured something out. You didn't have to take off."

I let out a relieved breath. "So am I in big trouble?" I bite my lip and hold my breath.

Mom sighs. "No. But you're going to call me every damn day while you're gone. And you come home right after that tour is over. No exceptions."

"Yes, ma'am."

"Tabitha, you really scared me tonight."

"I know, Mom. I'm sorry."

"Are the girls there? How is the tour going?"

Shit. Her acquiescence is all based on her assumption that I'm with the band. I wrack my brain for a suitable and believable lie. "Um, they're wiped out. I think everyone went to bed already."

"Oh, of course," she says. "Well, tell them all I said to break a leg."

I roll my eyes. "That's theatre, Mom."

"Right. Well, still. Tell them I said good luck, okay? And get some sleep. You sound exhausted."

"I will. Love you."

"Love you, too. And call me tomorrow."

I hang up the phone and notice the other traveler is staring at me. The security guard is nowhere in sight. I hug my backpack to my chest and make a mad dash for the bathroom. At least in there I have a door that locks.

I STAY IN THE BATHROOM most of the night. The bus for Champaign leaves at six, and when I go out to the waiting room at five-thirty, it's already filling up. By the time the bus pulls in, at least forty people are waiting. I don't see the man who scared me last night. I breathe a sigh of relief and take a seat. Exhaustion sets in fast, and I begin to doze. I'm so out of it that I almost miss the bus.

When I board, the only empty seat is next to a woman who seems be in her forties, maybe fifties. I'm bad with ages. She has a short haircut that's graying at the temples and gives me a friendly smile when I approach.

"Anyone sitting here?"

"Just you, honey." She pats the seat. I'm glad my travel companion isn't someone creepy. She looks like someone's friendly aunt.

"Thanks." I ease my way into the tiny seat, trying not to bump her with my broad hips.

"Where you headed?"

"Champaign."

"Business or pleasure?" Her voice is loud and boisterous, as though she doesn't seem to care if everyone on the bus can hear her.

"Um, both I guess. My friends are in a band that's playing a gig there tomorrow."

"Well, that sounds like fun." She smacks herself on the forehead. "I'm an idiot. I didn't even introduce myself." She holds out a hand. "I'm Diane Butterfield. Pleased to meet you."

"Tabitha," I reply, accepting her outstretched hand and giving it a halfhearted shake. Diane lifts a finger to her nose and gives it a twitch. I resist the urge to roll my eyes. "Yep, named for the TV witch."

"I love it!" Diane beams at me. "I'm named for an aunt I never met. Your namesake is definitely better."

I scoff. I've come to terms with my name, but it's far from being a name I would have picked. "Thanks, I guess."

I lean forward to shove my backpack under the seat, and Diane grabs my arm. "Let me see that pin," she demands.

I tilt the backpack in her direction and she squints, probably trying to read the small print on my "Smash the patriarchy" pin.

"I had a pin exactly like this," she says, pointing to the one that has a Venus symbol with a raised fist inside.

"Really?" I raise an eyebrow. This woman who looks almost old enough to be my grandmother was a feminist? And an angry one at that.

"I wasn't always this incredibly boring old lady," she says with a laugh. "Back in my day I was active with NOW and burned my bra with the best of them."

I raise my eyebrows. "That's so cool! Do you still protest and stuff?"

"Nah, I hung up my picket sign a long time ago." She sighs as if she's reminiscing. "Those were the days, though."

"So why'd you quit?"

She turns and studies me, as if she's sizing me up and deciding if I'm worthy of this particular part of her tale. She nods once, which I suppose is her deciding I might measure up.

"Are you sure you want to know?"

"Yeah. Did something happen?"

"Look, you seem like a sweet kid, and maybe you're not judgmental like girls were when I was your age."

I like to think I'm not judgmental, but, dear God, the suspense is killing me. What on earth could she possible have to tell me that might incite judgement or scorn on my part?

"The long and short of it is that I'm a lesbian."

I try to keep my expression neutral, but I am a bit shocked, and well, there is that complete lack of a poker face. "And that was a problem?"

"It shouldn't have been, but yeah, it was a big problem. Plus, I was dating this Indian girl, Tani."

"Why would that matter?"

"I loved my feminist sisters, but they weren't always accepting of people with differences."

Confused, I scrunch up my face. That doesn't make sense. Why would a group of women discriminate against other women when they were fighting for equality?

"Believe me, the irony wasn't lost on me," Diane says with a sardonic laugh. "We got called dykes a lot. And I don't think we won any fans being in an interracial relationship." She looks out the window at the farmland rolling by. "We got asked to leave the organization. I think the prevailing sentiment was that Middle America wasn't ready for all that *and* women's lib too." She shrugs. "Maybe they weren't."

"What happened with you and Tani?"

Without looking at me, Diane shakes her head. "We broke up not long after that. I think the pressure was too much for her. I can't imagine what that must have been like for her."

We fall silent. I'm not sure what Diane is thinking, but I'm thinking about Jackie. I don't think I've ever truly considered that she might have issues with our relationship that I hadn't been aware of. I assumed people would judge us because we're two girls but I guess I hadn't considered that there might be other problems.

I am so stupid. And more anxious than ever to get to Champaign and talk to Jackie. I bite my fingernails down to the quick.

"You look upset, honey." I hadn't even realized Diane was no longer staring out the window. She pats my hand. "I'm sorry if I upset you."

"No." I swallow around a lump in my throat. "It's just that what you said really hit home for me."

Diane raises a graying eyebrow.

"I'm bi and my girlfriend Jackie, well… she's African American. I only just now realized that she must have been fighting society on two fronts. One because she's gay and the other because she's with me."

Diane nods. "Well, that means there's still work to do. It's funny how we can get in our own little bubbles and not really see the depth and breadth of the world. But don't beat yourself up too much. You realize it now, and the good news is you can talk to her about it. I didn't have that luxury with Tani. I realized it too late, and by then she was gone."

Regret washes over Diane's face, and I want to hug her but we're practically strangers. Instead, I do the second-best thing. I change the subject.

"So where are you headed?" I ask.

I take a packet of Pop-Tarts out of my bag and offer her one. She takes the frosted pastry and smiles.

"St. Louis. My son lives there."

"Your son?"

"Being gay doesn't condemn you to a life of loneliness, honey. And don't look so shocked. I used a sperm donor." Her laugh is melodious and contagious.

We spend the rest of the two-hour trip sharing stories of our lives, and by the time we arrive in Champaign I don't want to leave her side.

When I hesitate, she gently nudges me out of the seat, "Honey, you have to go talk to that girlfriend of yours. Don't keep her waiting." She smiles at me, and the wrinkles around her blue eyes deepen.

"I hope you have a safe trip," I tell her. "I wish there was a way for us to— Oh wait!" I dig in my bag for a copy of my zine. "Here. I write this and it's got my address on the back." I duck my head, expecting rejection. "If you want to write."

Diane beams at me. "Of course I do, honey. You take care." She pats me on the arm and I turn to leave. When I get off the bus, I wave at her and watch her face get smaller and smaller in the window as the bus pulls away.

♀♡♀ CHAPTER 19 ★★★

The venue in Champaign is easy enough to find. The Stray Cat is right next to the Illinois campus in a brightly colored building with Shut Up's name on the marquee. Unfortunately, it doesn't open for another ten hours. I wait at the Burger King across the street, but, after a while, the staff regards me with frequent glances and I'm worried they might call the cops. As disheveled as I am, I must look homeless. I've got some cash on me, so I figure I can splurge on some new clothes, especially since I've already worn most of what I brought with me.

Up the street from the venue I find a thrift store, where I buy a new shirt and a pair of sunglasses, since I stupidly forgot mine, and then I go to a coffee shop where I'll look less out of place if I'm loitering.

In the back, sitting on a green pleather couch with her feet up on a low table is Jackie, flanked by Venus and Cherie. My heart flutters because I must have the best luck of anyone in the entire state of Illinois.

I take two steps in their direction when I hear someone shriek my name. I turn to face my assailant and come face to face with Marty. She has a new piercing in her left nostril and a tattoo of the band's name at her collarbone. Her hair is platinum blonde, which makes her look like an entirely different person, but there's no mistaking it, she's still Marty.

"Fucking A, Tabitha, that is some purple hair." She pulls me into a tight hug. "I didn't know you were coming on tour with us! Jacks said you had to work."

"I got fired," I say. Then I add, "For the hair."

She pulls back from her death grip and gives me a wide-eyed look of admiration. "That's so punk rock! I knew you had it in you," she says, grinning broadly. "Jackie is going to be so happy to see you. She's been talking about you nonstop." My face flushes as Marty throws her arm over my shoulders and leads me to the group.

Jackie practically leaps from the couch and throws her arms around me. I lift her off the ground and spin her.

"Oh my God, you two are disgustingly cute." Cherie presses her hands to her cheeks.

Venus looks a little tired—I have a feeling Marty may be on her worst behavior—but she smiles anyway. Her hair is different too, but I can't put my finger on it.

Jackie and I finally release each other but remain standing close. "How did you get here?" Jackie asks.

"The bus," I say. "I tried to make it to Peoria last night but there was an accident that closed down the highway so I got in too late. Then I had to wait until the next morning for a bus to Champaign."

"I can't believe you're here," Jackie gushes.

"I can hardly believe it myself," I admit. "Can we talk?" I whisper into Jackie's ear. Her eyes narrow, but she nods.

"Oh, no," Marty says. "You are not running off to make out or whatever. We were just getting ready to talk band business and plan our next issue of the zine."

"We can spare Jackie," Venus says.

"She's in charge of the zine," Marty says. "How can we plan it if she's not here?"

"It's all right," I say. "Jackie and I can talk later. It's nothing major."

Jackie glances in my direction, and I smile to reassure her. Marty gives Venus a smug smile and plops down in a cushy chair facing the green couch. Cherie moves to the other chair to give me the spot on the couch next to Jackie. I twine my fingers with hers, and she rests her ankle against mine. Her skin is warm and soft, and simply being next to her is a comfort. I feel like myself again.

"So Kate wants to write something for the zine about guitar picks or something. I don't know." Marty taps her pen on her notebook and looks to Jackie for her opinion.

"If she thinks it's relevant, I don't see why not," Jackie says.

Marty presses her lips together and makes a note of something.

I nudge Jackie with my elbow.

"Where is Kate?" I whisper.

"Sore subject. I'll tell you later." Jackie's breath is hot on my ear and it makes me squirm in my seat. I can't wait until this meeting is over and we can be alone. Jackie licks her lips as if she's thinking the same thing.

WHEN WE'RE FINALLY ALONE, IN what can only be described as a skeezy fleabag motel, Jackie and I can't keep our hands off each other. Her hands explore parts of my body we've never considered before. Okay, maybe I considered it, but we had always stopped short of… well, sex.

And that's the only word for what we're doing on an unmade bed in a random motel somewhere in Champaign, Illinois.

Her fingers are deft and nimble as they make my body come alive with desire. When she brings me over the edge, she kisses "I love you" into my skin. I fumble through mimicking her actions until they feel natural, and she moans my name into the afternoon haze of the room.

Blissed out and sleepy, we finally get a chance to talk.

"Did I hear you tell Marty you got fired?" Jackie's voice is a husky tenor, a sign she's on the verge of sleep.

I close my eyes and giggle as I nod. "My hair was a violation of the company dress code."

"Rebel girl." Jackie presses a soft kiss into my shoulder.

"That's me," I say with a laugh. "I dye my hair and skip town."

Jackie lifts her head. "You didn't tell your mom?"

"I left a note," I say, "and then called her last night."

"Was she pissed?"

"At first, but then she was cool with it. I kind of feel bad about not telling her before I left, you know? She sounded pretty worried about me."

Jackie bites her lip but doesn't say anything. She's probably as tired as I am.

"So what's up with Kate?" I ask, my eyes drifting closed even as I try to compel them to stay open.

Jackie sighs and curls into me. I quietly thrill at her warm breast touching the skin of my arm.

"Kate is seeing a guy in Donkey Kart that Marty has a crush on. When Marty caught them making out, it caused a fight, and now the two won't hang out unless it's for rehearsal or a show."

"Let me guess, this is mostly Marty's fault?"

"Got it in one," Jackie says with a yawn.

I try to think of something else to say, but my brain has finally shut down. I drift off in the comfort of Jackie's arms.

WE WAKE IN THE LATE afternoon to a pounding at the door.

"Wake up, bitches!" Marty shouts. "It's showtime."

Jackie rolls to her stomach and pulls a pillow over her head.

"We could stay here if you want." I pull the sheet from her legs and run my hand up the back of her thigh.

Marty knocks again. "You guys better be decent, because I'm coming in."

The key jiggles in the lock more than is necessary. I take the opportunity to pull the sheet over us.

"Come in," I tell her.

Jackie is still buried under her pillow. I nudge her with my foot, and she groans. "Five more minutes."

"Marty's here," I say.

"And we're leaving in ten," Marty adds. "Or you losers could stay in Champaign for the rest of your lives."

I give Marty my most threatening glare. "We're coming. Just give us a minute."

When she's gone, I roll toward Jackie and kiss her neck. "Come on. As nice as the last few hours have been, I don't want to live here."

Jackie chuckles and tosses her pillow at me.

♀♡♀ CHAPTER 20 ★★★

Shut Up has definitely improved since their first show at Decker Spring Fest. I can't believe it's the same group. Cherie has lost most of her stage fright and screams into the microphone with abandon. Kate and Venus seemed to be in complete sync, and Marty's riffs seem more polished, less rushed. I realize how much I've actually changed, too. I'm not the same person I was even a few months ago, and then again, I sort of am. It's a strange sensation.

Jackie winds her arm around my waist and presses her lips to my ear. "You're thinking too hard," she says. "Relax and enjoy the show." She kisses my cheek and trails her hand down my arm before taking my hand. She tugs gently and dances around me. She keeps tugging until I join her.

Dancing with abandon has always been my favorite way to relieve stress, and tonight is no exception. The last remnants of my unease over getting fired and my worry that Mom would be pissed about me taking off escape through my fingertips as I thrash.

At first it doesn't register because we're all moshing pretty hard. But after the fourth hit, I turn to look at the person who keeps ramming into my left shoulder. A guy with Billy Idol-blond hair towers over me; his slashed shirt and jeans expose strips of pale, white skin. He slams into me again, knocking me into Jackie. She stumbles and grabs my arm to steady herself.

"Watch it," I tell our Billy Idol wannabe.

"You watch it, lard-ass." He sneers and slams into me again.

This time the force of it knocks Jackie to the floor. She jumps to her feet and confronts the guy as best she can at half his size.

"What's your problem?" she shouts over the music.

I don't hear his answer over Marty shouting into the mic, "Down front some asshole is harassing our fellow Riot Grrrls. Everyone come forward and get this guy out of here. Blond hair, black Ramones shirt!"

The bouncer shoves forward with the crush of bodies on the dance floor and grabs the guy by the shoulders. As tall as Billy Idol Light is, the bouncer is bigger and more muscular and easily drags the guy off. Even so, he flails and spits and yells profanities at us. But the word he shouts at Jackie makes everything else seem like a loving endearment.

I've never heard someone called that in real life before. I know it happens, and I've heard it—movies, TV, music—but this is different altogether. I can't move and I can't read Jackie's reaction.

"Yeah, that's right! You're out of here," Marty yells. Then the band transitions into their next song as if nothing has happened.

Jackie tugs my arm until I start dancing again. But I can't get into it the way I had before. That guy shook me up.

Later, Jackie doesn't bring up the incident. So I do.

"What would you think about skipping the show tonight?" I ask her on the way to Terre Haute. We're in the back of the van. Kate's driving and the other girls are all asleep. "We could go to a movie or something. I think I have enough money left for that." I reach for my backpack.

"Why? Don't you want to go to the show?" She narrows her eyes and studies my face.

"Well, it's eighteen and up," I say, rooting through my backpack for my wallet. "So I figured you'd want to spend the evening with me."

"Oh, I forgot to tell you. Marty's got a fake ID you can use."

"That's great," I say, but I don't mean it. I wanted to keep Jackie away from the concert tonight in case that jerk from the night before decides to show up again. Terre Haute's only about an hour and a half from Champaign. It's not unreasonable, especially since he got kicked out. What if he's looking for revenge? "Actually, I'm not comfortable with using a fake ID. What if I get caught?"

Jackie rolls her eyes. "You won't get caught."

I bite my lip. Maybe I'll have to go with the truth. I pretend to count the money in my wallet and try to sound as nonchalant as possible. "What if that guy shows up?"

"What guy?"

"The one from last night. The one who called you a—"

"Stop right there," Jackie interrupts. "We are not running scared. And besides, I doubt that guy is going to follow us all the way to Indiana."

"It's not that far," I say. The wildflower-covered median goes by in a multicolored blur. We're already more than halfway to our destination.

"Okay, so he shows up. We'll get security to throw him out again."

"And if he waits for us after the show?"

Jackie lets out a frustrated breath. "Tabitha, I can't run away scared every time some jerk is a racist asshole. I'd hardly ever leave the house."

"But—" She presses a single finger to my lips.

"I've been dealing with idiots like him my whole life. Trust me."

I nod solemnly. Maybe she's right. Still, I can't shake the feeling that we're not safe.

AS THE TIME FOR THE show approaches, my anxiety kicks into overdrive. I don't know why Jackie is fighting me on this. Maybe I'm being unreasonable; maybe I'm overreacting, but it's only one show.

"Jackie, please let's do something else tonight," I beg. I'm sitting on the edge of the bed in the motel room we're sharing with Venus and Kate. Neither of them wanted to room with Marty, so Cherie gets her own bed. She seemed pretty happy about it. I wish I could be as carefree as the rest of them.

"Tabitha, you're being ridiculous." Jackie chuckles as she checks her teeth in the mirror, but I can tell she's frustrated with me. She picks up her toothbrush, and I hear the faucet spring to life.

"Why is it so important for you to go to this show? There are a dozen more just like it. You won't miss anything."

"It's the principle," she says around a mouth full of toothpaste. "I made a commitment and I'm sticking to it. Vee wants me there, and I agreed to work the merch table tonight. So you can go with me or you can stay here and mope. But I'm going." She spits into the sink and rinses, then slams her toothbrush on the counter. Without another word, she leaves the room and me.

I want to go after her, but I also need some time to figure out what's actually going on with me. Why am I so scared of one guy?

I try to remember the feeling from last night when we got shoved. My pulse quickens and my breathing becomes more shallow as I feel the memory: Jackie's face as she staggered backward and the guy's anger when Jackie yelled back. I've never seen that kind of look on someone's face before. It was pure hate. And he didn't even know us. Has she been faced with that kind of hostility her whole life?

I try to imagine Jackie as a little girl, or her little sister Janae, getting harassed by our low-rent Billy Idol and I can't. What would possess someone to treat a child like that? Just because of their skin color? It doesn't make any sense.

It may sound foolish, but for the first time in my life I realize what a sheltered life I've lived. Jackie has experienced the world in a completely different way than I have, and that's only now occurring to me. I've always known intellectually that this kind of thing happened, but I never gave it much thought. No wonder she was angry with me. I would be too. I've been a complete moron. How could I have been so blind? Now our fight before she left Decker makes sense.

I search wildly for my shoes. I need to talk to Jackie.

I FIND KATE HANGING WITH the Donkey Kart guys and Cherie is with Mark. Marty is sitting on the hood of the van, working on a new song. Her guitar is across her lap, and she periodically leans forward to jot something in her notebook. Venus tells me she saw Jackie head in the direction of the front desk, but when I get there I find a greasy-looking man behind the desk eating a sandwich. Where did she go?

After several more minutes of frantic searching, I find a dazed Jackie sitting on the curb near a pay phone. She's drinking a Pepsi and staring off into the distance. She looks like she's been crying.

"There you are. I've been looking everywhere for you. I wanted to apologize. I didn't realize…" Jackie smiles at me but a tear rolls down her cheek. "What's wrong? Is there something else?"

"I'm leaving," she says. "I'm going back to Decker."

My stomach drops out. She's breaking up with me. "What? Why?" I plop down beside her on the curb.

"I talked to my mom," she says. Her voice is thick and watery.

"Is everything okay? Janae… is she all right?"

"Everything's fine, Tabitha." Jackie smiles broadly and looks me square in the eye. "Mom wants me to come home. To stay."

I throw my arms around her. "Jackie, that's great!"

"When I stormed off, I called home. I don't know why. I had this overwhelming urge to talk to my mom. I'd been thinking about her a lot—ever since you told me about your mom's reaction when you called her." Jackie looks off into the distance, and her eyes fill with tears. "When I took off, I didn't tell her where I was going. She didn't know where I was for about a week until she ran into Vee's mom at the grocery store." She sniffs. "She told me she loved me and said she was glad I was safe."

"And the gay thing?"

Jackie shrugs. "She's still not happy about it, but she's willing to work on it if I come home."

"Jackie, that's wonderful."

"So I'm heading out tonight."

"Oh." I stare at my feet and try to hide my disappointment. I know this is the right thing for her, but I just got here and I wanted to spend the next couple of weeks with her.

She shoves my shoulder playfully. "I want you to come with me, silly."

"Really?"

She kisses me instead of responding.

When she pulls away my mind is already racing. "I need to call my mom and get us bus tickets. And we need to tell the girls. What about the zine? Marty's going to be pissed."

"I'll let Vee handle Marty. You call your mom, and I'll get packed."

She gives me another soft kiss and then she's gone. My fingers fumble as I dial my home number.

We're mostly quiet on the bus ride back to Decker. I have so much I want to say to Jackie, but she seems as though she's about to bubble over from excitement. I don't want to dull that.

On her lap, Jackie's holding a tiny stuffed cat that she bought for Janae. She hasn't put it down since she picked it up in the convenience store next to our motel, when she went in for some snacks for the trip and came out with the artificial calico cat under her arm.

I'm nervous about meeting her family, but I'm so happy for her I could burst. I can tell she's nervous too, but she won't stop smiling.

"Are you okay with heading back early?" Jackie asks. "I know you were excited about the tour."

"I was excited about spending time with you. Still doing that."

She caresses my cheek. I can tell she wants to kiss me, but I know she won't in public. Not when we don't know anyone. I want to kiss her too, so I squeeze her hand for reassurance. She squeezes back.

After a few moments I decide it's time we talked. "I really am sorry about earlier," I say, knowing it's not enough but hoping it does the job.

Jackie waves me off. "It's fine. I know you were just worried about me." She turns to gaze out the window. "But you have to understand, that kind of stuff is going to happen. And some of it may even be directed at you."

"How do you deal with it?"

"Lifetime of practice. Parents who talked to me about that stuff."

"I'm sorry I was such an idiot. I didn't realize what it's like for you."

"You got a lot to learn, babe."

"I know. And I will."

WAITING AT THE BUS STATION is a woman I recognize from graduation: Jackie's mom, Deborah. Her skin is a darker brown than Jackie's, but they have the same delicate nose and high cheekbones. On her hip is a small boy with long, skinny legs and a toothless grin. Standing next to them is a slightly smaller version of Jackie with shoulder-length braids adorned at the ends with pink beads. Janae is holding on to the last vestiges of childhood, but it's evident that puberty isn't far off. When she sees Jackie, she waves and bounces on her feet. The little boy, Jackson, wriggles from his mother's arms and does the same. The moment we're off the bus both children race for her and throw their arms around her. Mrs. Hardwick smiles with closed lips as tears fill her eyes.

Jackie frees herself from her siblings' grip and takes a few tentative steps toward her mother.

"Hi, Mama."

"Hello, Jacqueline."

They stare at each other, and I think the tension is going to boil over. But then Jackie breaks into a huge smile and throws her arms around her mother. Deborah's arms drift up to Jackie's shoulders, and her eyes close as tears begin to fall.

"You're home, baby girl," she says softly. "You're home at last."

Jackie pulls away and wipes her eyes. She gestures for me to come forward. "Mama, I want you to meet my girlfriend, Tabitha."

I hold out my hand. "Hello, Mrs. Hardwick. It's nice to meet you."

She stares at my palm with a furrowed brow. Oh God, she's going to snub me. Maybe I shouldn't have dyed my hair. Maybe Jackie shouldn't have introduced me as her girlfriend right out of the gate. I wriggle my fingers nervously and start to pull away. Then she smiles. "I'm a hugger, Tabitha. So you better get used to it." She wraps her thick arms around me and squeezes. "Ooh, this girl has some meat on her bones. You could learn a thing or two from her."

Over Mrs. Hardwick's shoulder I see Jackie's bright smile and I return it, full force.

"I love you," I mouth.

Her lips form the same words as her mother releases me.

"Well, let's get out of here. I made pot roast for dinner and if we don't get home soon, Jerome will eat it all."

Jackie's sidelong glance tells me she's worried about Jerome's reaction, but there's also determination in her eyes. She's not about to let anyone make her feel like less of a person. Not even her brother.

I laugh at myself. How could I have ever worried about her? She's going to be fine.

We're going to be fine.

♥GRRRLS ON THE SIDE NO. 1

Welcome to Grrrls on the Side, a zine created by Jackie Hardwick and Venus Jones. We're a couple of gorgeous badass goddesses and it's time someone heard from us. So sit back and enjoy the ride because you're about to get a reality check from the sidelines. But we won't be on the sidelines for long. We're sick and tired of not being allowed to be love interests. We want to be the main characters of our own stories.

A Gap in the Pay Gap as told by Venus Jones

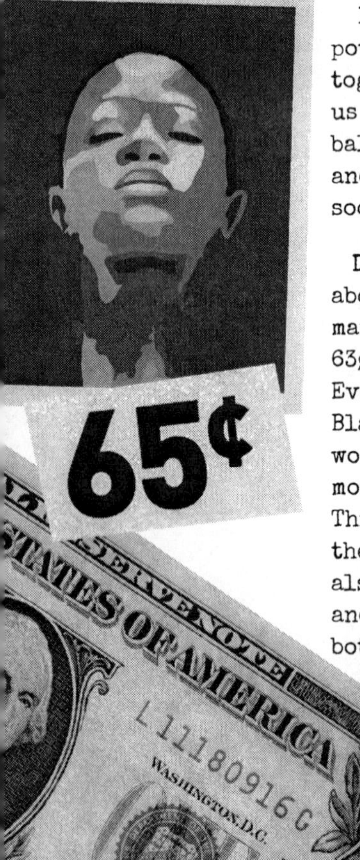

I hear a lot of grrrls talk about girl power and that women need to stick together but when it comes to including us brown and black girls, y'all drop the ball. Feminism isn't just for white girls and the sooner everyone realizes that, the sooner we'll get what we want.

Did you know that white women make about 70¢ on the dollar to what a white man makes? And a black woman makes about 63¢ and a Hispanic woman makes about 55¢? Even men aren't exempt from this racism. Black men barely make more than white women and Hispanic men barely eke out more than black women. Wake up, people! This is a systemic issue. We need to close the pay gap across gender lines, but it's also about race. Stop ignoring my color and separating it from my gender. I am both things at once.

MENDING FENCES AND FIXING YOUR WEAVE

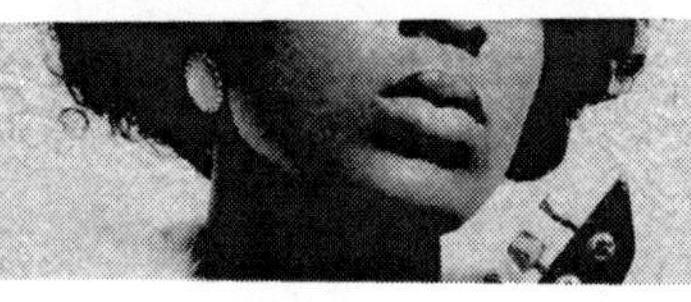

Redemption can be a powerful thing. I never thought I'd say it but I'm happy to be back home. I spent the early part of the summer on tour with Shut Up and let me tell you, my girl Venus can tear up a beat. But I was homesick and I didn't realize it.

I've mended relationships and apologized for my errors. I've forgiven and asked for forgiveness. It's not been an easy road, but life is good.

Don't get me wrong. Life isn't perfect. Yesterday my girlfriend said to me, "I wish I could grow my hair long enough to do braids like that," and I had to explain a weave to her.

She's got a lot to learn. But we're working on it.

~Jackie

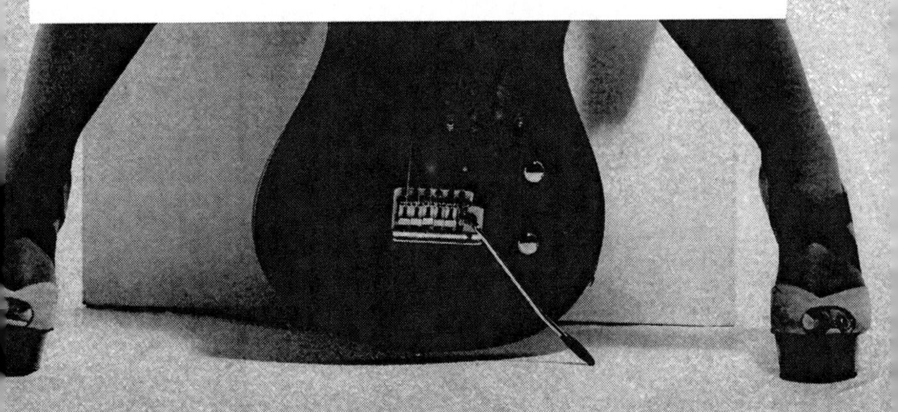

ACKNOWLEDGMENTS

This book would not exist without the influence of many powerful women in my life. First and foremost, my mother, who taught me my worth existed beyond my body. Also my grandmother, who taught me that I could make my voice heard. She was born before women could vote and worked tirelessly in politics and social causes throughout her life. She was a true Riot Grrrl and I will be forever grateful that I got to call her *my* Granny.

I would also like to thank my editor and good friend Annie Harper. She makes my books shine and pushes me to believe in myself even when I want to give up. It's an invaluable friendship and working relationship that I am extremely lucky to have. I also want to thank Nicki and Zoe. You continually challenge me to write more concisely and it makes my writing better.

To the wonderful Ebony and Wesaun, thank you for pushing me to look beyond myself and my personal experience to make *Grrrls* a book that anyone can enjoy.

I also owe a huge thanks to everyone else at Interlude Press—CL Miller, CB Messer, and the late Lex Huffman. This book is a result of the guidance and talent you've shared with me over the years.

To Brian Brewer, my best friend and an honorary Riot Grrrl, thanks for letting me be catty and crude whenever I need to. But for also cheerleading and critiquing my writing. To Knits, a lovely soul whose friendship and support means so much. I think our 1994 versions would have been friends who joined Riot Grrrl together. To Laura Stone, thank you for being a dear friend, mentor, beta and all-around awesome lady. To my fellow authors who publish with Interlude Press and Duet Books, thanks for being a part of this supportive group of talented writers who believe in diverse fiction.

And to my husband, Josh, a true feminist and supporter of women's rights, you are the best thing that's ever come into my life. Thank you for knowing that I need support, love, and truth—even when I don't want to admit it. You make me stronger and a better person, and I love you beyond words.

ABOUT THE AUTHOR

Never one for following the "rules," Carrie Pack is a published author of books in multiple genres, including *Designs on You* (2014) and *In the Present Tense* (2016). Her novels focus on characters finding themselves in their own time—something she experienced for herself when she came out as bisexual recently. She's passionate about positive representation in her writing and has been a feminist before she knew what the word meant thanks to a progressive and civic-minded grandmother. Coincidentally, that's also where she got her love of red lipstick and desserts. Carrie lives in Florida, or as she likes to call it, "America's Wang."

@duet**books**

Twitter | Tumblr

*For a reader's guide to **Grrrls on the Side** and book club prompts, please visit duetbooks.com.*

Also by **Carrie Pack**

In the Present Tense

Published by Interlude Press

Miles Lawson goes to sleep dreaming of a future with his boyfriend Adam, but wakes to find he is married to Ana, an acquaintance from high school. When he learns he has been time traveling, Miles is consumed with finding a cure for his rare condition—and finding his first love. But will he be able to convince Adam he is telling the truth before it's too late?

ISBN (print) 978-1-941530-78-8 | (eBook) 78-1-941530-79-5

Designs On You

Published by Interlude Press

If graphic artist Scott Parker designs one more cupcake logo, he might lose it. When asked to retouch photos for a fashion client, a stunning model occupies his fantasies long after the job is done. The model is soon assigned to one of Scott's projects, and Scott struggles to overcome Jamie Donovan's aloof manner. Will Jamie follow through on Scott's interest, or is he just an untouchable fantasy?

ISBN (print) 978-1-941530-04-7 | (eBook) 978-1-941530-14-6

You may **also** like...

The Seafarer's Kiss by Julia Ember

Published by Duet, an imprint of Interlude Press

After rescuing the maiden Ragna, mermaid Ersel realizes the life she wants is above the sea. But when Ersel's suitor catches them together, she must say goodbye or face brutal justice from the king. Desperate, Ersel makes a deal with Loki and is exiled as a result. To fix her mistakes and be reunited with Ragna, Ersel must outsmart the God of Lies.

ISBN (print) 978-1-945053-20-7 | (eBook) 978-1-945053-34-4

CPSIA information can be obtained
at www.ICGtesting.com
Printed in the USA
LVOW11s1006120817
544677LV00002B/1/P